"Now… my terms for marriage."

Olympia's eyes opened very wide and she froze.

"*Yes*. What you want is within reach, but you may yet choose not to pay the price."

"The price?"

"All good things come at a price…haven't you learned that yet?" Nik murmured in a voice as smooth and rich as honey.

LYNNE GRAHAM was born in Northern Ireland and has been a keen Harlequin reader since her teens. She is very happily married to an understanding husband, who has learned to cook since she started to write! Her five children keep her on her toes. She has a very large Old English sheepdog, which knocks everything over, and two cats. When time allows, Lynne is a keen gardener.

Lynne Graham

THE COZAKIS BRIDE

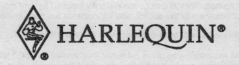

HARLEQUIN®

TORONTO • NEW YORK • LONDON
AMSTERDAM • PARIS • SYDNEY • HAMBURG
STOCKHOLM • ATHENS • TOKYO • MILAN • MADRID
PRAGUE • WARSAW • BUDAPEST • AUCKLAND

ISBN 0-373-12103-2

THE COZAKIS BRIDE

First North American Publication 2000.

Visit us at www.eHarlequin.com

Printed in U.S.A.

CHAPTER ONE

'YOU have ruined your life just as your mother did,' Spyros Manoulis condemned.

Olympia studied her Greek grandfather with shuttered eyes the colour of sea jade. She was sick with nerves but she had come on a begging mission. If venting his spleen put the older man into a better mood and made him look more sympathetically on her mother's plight, she could stand the heat of any attack.

Well-built and fit, for all his seventy-plus years, the white-haired older man paced the lounge of his luxurious London hotel suite, his lined features forbidding. 'Look at you, still single at the age of twenty-seven! No husband, no children,' he cited grimly. 'Ten years ago, I opened my home to you and I attempted to do my best for you...'

As he paused for a necessary breath, broad chest expanding, Olympia *knew* what was coming next. Beneath the mahogany hair she wore confined in a French plait, her pallor became pronounced.

'And how was my generosity repaid?' Spyros was working himself up into a rage at the memory. 'You brought dishonour on the family name. You disgraced me, destroyed your own reputation and offered unforgivable insult to the Cozakis family—'

'Yes...' Olympia was desperate enough to own up to murder itself if it calmed her grandfather down and gave her the chance to plead her mother's cause.

'Such a marriage as I arranged for you...and very grateful you were to have Nikos Cozakis at the time! You wept when he gave you your betrothal ring. I remember the occasion well!'

Olympia clenched her teeth together: a necessary self-restraint. Hot, cringing humiliation was eating into her self-discipline.

'Then you threw it all away in a wanton moment of madness,' Spyros Manoulis ground out with bitter anger. 'Shamed me, shamed yourself—'

Olympia whispered tautly, 'Ten years is a long time—'

'Not long enough to endow me with forgetfulness!' her grandfather countered harshly. 'I was curious to see you again. That's why I agreed to this meeting when you wrote asking for it. But let me tell you now without further waste of time that you will receive no financial assistance from me.'

Olympia reddened. 'I want nothing for me...but my mother, your daughter—'

Spyros interrupted her before she could mention her mother's name. 'Had my foolish daughter raised you to be a decent young woman, according to our Greek traditions, you would *never* have brought dishonour upon me!'

At that judgmental assurance, Olympia's heart sank. So her innocent parent was still to suffer for her daughter's sins. Squaring her slim shoulders, she lifted a chin every bit as determined as his own. '*Please* let me speak freely—'

'No, I will not hear you!' Spyros stalked over to the window. 'I want you to go home and think about what you have lost for you and your mother. *Had* you married Nik Cozakis—'

'I'd have castrated him!' Olympia's control over her temper slipped as the older man made it clear that their meeting was already at an end.

Her grandfather's beetling brows rose almost as high as his hairline.

Olympia coloured. 'I'm sorry—'

'At least Nik would have taught you to keep a still tongue when a man is speaking to you!'

Olympia sucked in a deep, steadying breath. He was as mad as fire now. She had done nothing but add fuel to the flames. No doubt she ought to have arrived steeped in sack-cloth and ashes and hung her head with anguished regret when he referred to her broken engagement.

Spyros Manoulis moved his hand in a gesture of finality. 'You could only win my forgiveness by marrying Nik.'

Fierce disappointment filled Olympia to overflowing. 'Why don't you just throw in climbing Everest too?'

'I see you get the picture,' her grandfather said drily.

But there was a little red devil buzzing about now inside Olympia's head. 'If I could get him to marry me, would I still come dowered with the Manoulis empire?'

The older man dealt her a thunderous appraisal. 'What are you suggesting? *Get* him to marry you? Nikos Cozakis, whom you insulted beyond belief, who could have any young woman he wanted—'

'Few young women come with as large a dowry as you offered as a sweetener to the deal over me ten years ago.'

Spyros Manoulis was aghast at her bluntness. 'Have you no shame?'

'When you tried to flog me off like one of your tankers, I lost my illusions and my sensitivity,' his granddaughter asserted curtly. 'You still haven't answered my question.'

'But what is the point of a question that crazy?' The older man flung both hands up in complete exasperation.

'I'd just like to know.'

'I would have signed control of Manoulis Industries over to Nik on your wedding day…and I would *still* gladly do so, were it possible!' Weary now, his big shoulders slumping, Spyros vented an embittered laugh at what he saw as a total impossibility. 'My only desire was to pass on the business I spent a lifetime building into capable hands. Was that so much to ask?'

Olympia's generous mouth compressed. The longevity of his name in the business world meant so much more to her grandfather than family ties. But then to be fair that was not her gentle mother's view. Irini Manoulis might long to be reconciled with her estranged father, but the older woman had never blamed him for turning his back on her. However, an increasing sense of despair was creeping over Olympia. Her grandfather was immovable. He had admitted to only seeing her out of curiosity. So why was she still hanging around where she wasn't welcome?

Olympia walked stiff-backed to the door and then decided to make one last attempt to be heard. 'My mother's health is failing—'

Spyros growled something at her in outraged Greek, his refusal to listen instantaneous.

Olympia spun back, sea-jade eyes flashing like gems. 'If she dies poor and miserable, as she is now, I hope your conscience haunts you to the grave and beyond, because that's what you'll deserve!'

For a second, Spyros Manoulis stared at her with expressionless dark eyes. Then he swung away, his broad back stiff as an iron bar.

Leaving her grandfather's suite, Olympia got into the lift before she slumped. Minutes later, having got herself back under control, she crossed the busy hotel foyer back out into the open air. Maybe she should run really insane and kidnap Nik Cozakis, she thought with enormous bitterness. If she'd had the money she could have hired hitmen to snatch him out of his stretch limo. And she could have personally starved and tortured Nik in some dark, dank cellar with a completely clear conscience. After all, she hated him. She really, really hated him.

Although already wealthy beyond avarice, greed had led Nik at the age of nineteen into getting engaged to a plain, overweight girl who'd had no attraction for him *but* her value as the promised Manoulis heiress. Nik Cozakis had broken her heart, dragged her pride in the dirt and ultimately ensured that there was no prospect of Spyros *ever* forgiving either her or her mother.

But then maybe her mother had been born under an unlucky star, Olympia conceded, wincing at the hardness of the pavement beneath shoe soles worn thin as paper with overuse. For the first twenty-one years of her life Irini had been cocooned in a world of wealth and privilege. Then she had made the fatal mistake of falling in love with an Englishman. Meeting with heavy paternal opposition, Irini had fled to London to be with her boyfriend. But the day before their wedding was to take place Olympia's father had crashed his motorbike and died.

Shortly afterwards, Irini had discovered that she was pregnant. From that point on there had been no turning back: she was expecting a child and she was unmarried. Her only talent a willingness to take any manual work available, Irini had raised Olympia alone. Throughout her childhood, Olympia could only recall her mother with a wan, exhausted face, for Irini Manoulis had never been strong. And the reality was that all those years of taxing physical labour had wrecked what health she did have and weakened her heart.

Once Olympia had been old enough to get a job of her own, matters had improved. For a few years, Olympia recalled with painful regret, they had been happy in a tiny flat which had seemed like a palace to them both. Then, eighteen months ago, the firm where Olympia had worked as a receptionist had gone bankrupt. Since then she had only managed to get temporary employment, and even that had been thin on the ground in recent months. They had had to give up the flat, and the savings which Olympia had painstakingly built up were long since gone.

The council had rehoused them in a tough inner city estate. Her mother was so terrified of the aggressive youths there that she no longer dared to venture out. Olympia had been forced to watch the mother she adored decline before her eyes, growing ever more thin and weak, her brave smiles of cheer pathetic to witness. It was as if Irini Manoulis had given up on life itself.

She was dying, Olympia reflected sickly, dying inch by

inch, always talking about the distant past now, because the unlovely present was too much for her weakened spirit to handle. A rundown apartment they couldn't afford to heat, no telephone, no television, noisy, threatening neighbours and surroundings bereft of all beauty. Nothing, nothing whatsoever to look forward to with the smallest anticipation.

If only Olympia had had the benefit of a crystal ball ten years ago...*if only*! Would she have made the same decision as she had made then? A despairing laugh was dredged from Olympia. Guilt and all the regret her grandfather could ever had wished on her washed over her now. She would have been married to a billionaire! Long before her health had failed her mother would once again have enjoyed security and comfort. Now, with bitter, realistic hindsight, Olympia knew that had she had the benefit of a crystal ball at the age of seventeen she would have married a monster for her mother's sake!

So what if Nik had been snogging the face off a gorgeous Italian model not ten feet from her?

So what if Nik had confided in his second cousin, Katerina, that Olympia was, 'Fat and stupid and sexless, but literally worth her weight in gold!'?

So what if he would have been continually unfaithful throughout their marriage and a total arrogant, loathsome pig to live with?

So what if he had said to her face, without scruple, conscience or decency, the morning after that dreadful night, 'You're a slapper! And I, Nik Cozakis, refuse to marry another man's leavings!'?

Gripped by those painfully degrading recollections, Olympia hovered by a shop window. She knew that right now Nik was sure to be over in London for the same reason as her grandfather was. It had featured in the newspapers: a meeting of powerful Greek tycoons with shared interests in British business. And, unlike Spyros Manoulis, Nik had a massive office headquarters in the City of London, where he very likely was this *very* minute...

What did she have to lose? He was still single. And Spyros Manoulis never joked about money. Spyros would happily pay millions and millions of pounds to marry her off to Nik Cozakis. Personalities didn't come into it: primarily it would be the linking of two enormous business empires. And with that size of a dowry still available, even a plain Jane slapper ought to have the gumption to put a late offer on the table! Was she crazy? No, she owed a huge debt to her mother. Irini Manoulis had sacrificed so much to bring her into the world and raise her to adulthood. What had *she* ever given back?

Olympia squinted at her reflection in the shop window. A dark-haired woman of five foot five inches, clad in a grey skirt and jacket shabby with age. Even on a restricted diet she was never going to be thin. Her shape was lush—horribly, embarrassingly lush. She must have inherited such generous curves from her father's side, because her mother was slim and slight. Well, she was worth her weight in gold, she reminded herself bracingly. And if there was one thing Nik Cozakis reputedly excelled at, it was ruthlessly exploiting any proposition likely to enrich his already overflowing coffers...

Nik was planning a major deal.

All calls were on hold, with only the direst emergency excuse for an interruption of any kind. So when even the softest of knocks sounded hesitantly on the door of his office his dark head came up, well-defined black brows rising in exasperated enquiry. His British PA, Gerry, hurried to the door, where a whispered exchange took place.

Gerry moved back to his powerful employer's side. 'I'm sorry, but there's a woman asking to see you urgently, sir.'

'No interruptions, particularly not of the female variety,' Nik cut in with harsh impatience.

'She says she's Spyros Manoulis's granddaughter, Olympia. But the receptionist isn't convinced of her identity. I gather the woman doesn't *look* like someone you would be acquainted with, sir.'

Olympia Manoulis? Arrested into tangible stillness, Nik Cozakis frowned in silent disbelief. Olympia Manoulis. Rooted deep in his subconscious lurked a tender spot still raw with a rage that had yet to dim. How dared that whore enter his office block and have the effrontery to ask to see him? He plunged upright, startling his staff so much that everybody jumped, and one unfortunate dropped several files.

Striding over to the tall tinted windows like a leopard on the prowl for fresh meat, Nik stilled again. Spyros had sworn he would never forgive her. Spyros was a man of his word. And Nik still pitied the older man, whose deep shame over his erring granddaughter's behaviour had been painful to witness. His only son had drowned in a yacht race and his daughter had become an unwed mother. Bad blood in that family, Nik's own father had decided, implying that his headstrong son had had a narrow escape.

Yet still Nik simmered like a boiling cauldron when he recalled the humiliation of being publicly confronted with the fact that *his* fiancée, *his* doe-eyed supposedly virginal bride-to-be, had gone out to *his car* with a drunken friend and had *sex* with him. It was disgusting; it was filthy. In fact, just thinking about that degrading, utterly inexcusable episode still had the power to make Nik regret that he had never had the opportunity to punish Olympia Manoulis as she had so definitely deserved.

The atmosphere was so explosive that the silence was absolute. His staff exchanged uncertain glances. Gerry Marsden waited, and then slowly breathed in. 'Sir…?'

Nik wheeled back. 'Let her wait…'

His PA concealed his surprise with difficulty. 'At what time will I tell your secretary that you will see her?'

'No time.' His eyes cold enough to light the way to Hades, Nik threw back his proud dark head. 'Let her *wait*.'

As the hours crept past into the lunch hour, and then on into the late afternoon, Olympia was conscious that quite a few people seemed to pass suspiciously slowly through the impressive reception area and steal a covert glance in her direction.

She held her head high, neck aching from that determined show of indifference. She had her foot in the door, she told herself bracingly. Nik hadn't had her escorted off the premises. Nik had not flatly refused to see her. And if he was very, very busy, that was only what she had expected, and she could not hope for any favours. Curiosity would eventually penetrate that arrogant, macho and bone-deep stubborn skull of his. Even Nik Cozakis had to be that human.

Despair was the mother of invention, she conceded. Nik Cozakis was literally her last hope. And why *should* her fierce pride hurt? No false pride had held her mother back from scrubbing other people's floors so that she could feed and clothe her daughter.

Just before five o'clock, the receptionist rose from behind her desk. 'Mr Cozakis has left the building, Miss Manoulis.'

Olympia paled to the colour of milk. Then she straightened her stiff shoulders and stood up. She stepped into the lift and let it carry her back down to the ground floor. She would be back tomorrow to keep the same vigil, she told herself doggedly. She would not be embarrassed into retreat by such tactics. But, even so, she was as badly shaken as if she had run into a hard brick wall.

As she stood on the bus that would eventually bring her within walking distance of home, she realised that she had read the situation wrong. Nik was no longer the teenager she had once been so pathetically infatuated with: impatient and hot-tempered, with not a lot in the way of self-control. The eldest son of two adoring parents, he had been the natural leader in his sophisticated social set of bored but gilded youth.

And so beautiful, so heartachingly, savagely beautiful that

it must have seemed like a crime to his unlovely friends that
he should be matched with an unattractive, plump and charm-
less bride-to-be...

But now Nik was a fully grown adult male. A *Greek* male,
subtly different from others of his sex. Like her grandfather,
he saw no need to justify his own behaviour. There had been
no quiet announcement that he was unavailable. He had *let*
her wait and cherish hope. That had been cruel, but she
should have been better prepared for that tack.

The scent of cooking greeted Olympia's return to the flat
she shared with her mother. She hurried into the tiny kitchen
and watched her mother gather her spare frame and turn with
a determined smile to greet her. Her heart turned over sickly
at the grey pallor of the older woman's worn face.

"I thought we agreed that *I* do all the cooking, Mum.'

'You've been out looking for a job all day. It's the least
that I can do,' Irini Manoulis protested.

Later, as Olympia climbed into bed, she was consumed by
guilt for the evasions she had utilised with her mother. But
how could she have told the older woman what she had *really*
been doing all day? Irini would have been upset by the
knowledge that her daughter had secretly got in touch with
her grandfather, but unsurprised by the outcome. However,
an admission that Olympia had tried to see Nik Cozakis
would have left her mother bereft of breath and a frank explanation of *why* her daughter had sought that meeting would
have appalled her quiet and dignified parent.

But how much more shattered would her trusting mother
have been had Olympia ever told her the whole dreadful truth
of what had happened in Athens a decade earlier? Olympia
had never told that story, and her awareness of that fact still
disturbed her. Then, as now, Olympia had kept her own
counsel to protect her mother from needless distress...

The next morning, Olympia took up position in the waiting
area on the top floor of the Cozakis building three minutes
after nine o'clock.

She made the same request to see Nik as she had made the day before. The receptionist avoided eye contact. Olympia wondered if *this* would be the day that Nik lost patience and had her thrown out of the building.

At ten minutes past nine, after a mutually mystified consultation with another senior member of staff, Gerry Marsden approached Nik, who had started work as usual at eight that morning. 'Miss Manoulis is here again today, sir.'

Almost imperceptibly the Greek tycoon tensed and the silence thickened.

'Have you the Tenco file?' Nik then enquired, as if the younger man hadn't spoken.

The day wore on, with Olympia praying that a pretence of quiet, uncomplaining humility would ultimately persuade Nik to spare her just five minutes of his time. By the end of that day, when the receptionist apologetically announced that Mr Cozakis had again left the building, Olympia experienced such a violent surge of bitter frustration that she could have screamed.

On the third day, Olympia felt hugely conspicuous as she stepped out of the lift on to the top floor.

Before leaving home she would have liked to have filled a vacuum flask and made herself some sandwiches, but to have done so would have roused her mother's suspicions and her concern. Since Olympia had yet to admit to her mother that their slender resources were now stretched unbearably tight. Irini fondly imagined that her daughter *bought* lunch for herself while she was out supposedly seeking employment.

However, at noon, when Olympia returned from a visit to the enviably luxurious cloakroom on the top floor, she found a cup of tea and three biscuits awaiting her. Her strained face softened with her smile. The receptionist gave her a decidedly conspiratorial glance in return. By then, Olympia was convinced that just about every person of importance in the building had traversed the reception area to take a peek at her. Sympathy was now softening the discomfiture her initial vigil had inspired. Not that it was going to do her much good, she conceded heavily, when Nik obviously had an alternative exit from his office.

At three that afternoon, when the last of her patience had worn away, her desperation started to mount. Nik would soon be on his way back to Greece and even more out of her reach. Olympia reached a sudden decision and got up swiftly from her seat. Hurrying past the reception desk that she had previously respected as a barrier, she started down the wide corridor that had to lead to Nik's inner sanctum.

'Miss Manoulis, you *can't* go down there!' the young receptionist exclaimed in dismay.

She would be a loser now whatever she did, Olympia reflected with despairing bitterness. Forcing a confrontation with Nik was the wrong line to take. No Greek male appreciated an in-your-face female challenge. He would react like a caveman, every aggressive primal cell outraged by such boldness.

As she headed for the door at the foot of the corridor, a set of male hands whipped round her forearms from behind and stopped her dead in her tracks.

'I'm sorry, Miss Manoulis, but nobody goes in there without the boss's say-so,' an accented Greek voice spelt out tautly.

'Damianos…' Even after ten years Olympia recognised that gravelly voice, and her rigid shoulders bowed in defeat. Nik's bodyguard, who was built like a tank. 'Couldn't you have looked the other way just once?'

'For your grandfather's sake, go home,' Damianos urged in a fierce undertone. '*Please* go home, before you are eaten alive.'

Olympia trembled as the older man's fingers loosened their

hold. But that reluctance on his part to treat her like any other unwanted visitor was Damianos's mistake. Breaking free without hesitation, she literally flung herself the last ten feet and burst through that door.

There was a blur of movement from behind the desk: Nik rising with startled abruptness at so explosive an interruption.

In the split second that she knew was all she had at her disposal before Damianos intervened again, with greater effect, Olympia parted her lips and breathed rawly, 'Are you a man or a mouse that you won't face one woman?'

CHAPTER TWO

FROM behind Olympia, Damianos read Nik's face and avoided seeing the slight inclination of his employer's head which signified his own dismissal.

Out of breath, and expecting at any minute to be dragged out again, Olympia focused on Nik Cozakis for the first time in ten long years. Shock shrilled through her. He had got taller, his shoulders wider, and he had been tall and wide even to begin with. Well over six feet, he had towered over his relatives and friends. Now he cast a shadow like an intimidating stone monolith.

Olympia could feel his outrage like a physical entity, churning up the heavy silence, beating down on her in suffocating waves. *Man or mouse?* A truly insane, derisive opening likely to push the average Greek male to violent response. She marvelled at his self-control, even as she winced at the loss of her own. Had she been a man, Nik would have knocked her through the wall for such an insult.

'I'm sorry,' Olympia said, though she wasn't one bit sorry.

'Damianos...' Nik murmured flatly.

The door behind her finally closed.

Olympia stared at him, couldn't help it. His sheer impact hit her and she reeled back an involuntary step, her tummy full of butterflies, her skin dampening. She took all of him in, all at once, in a single, almost greedy visualising burst. The devastating dark good looks, the raw, earthy force of his sexual aura, the contrasting formal severity of his beautifully cut dark suit. All male, nothing of the boy left but that aching beauty which had once entrapped her foolish heart. And those eyes, amber-gold as a jaguar cat, spectacularly noticeable in that lean, strong face.

18

'Why are you humiliating yourself in this way?' Nik enquired in a drawl as lazy as a hot summer afternoon.

Belatedly, Olympia recognised her disorientation for the weakness it was. Angry dismay trammelled through her. She dredged her dilated pupils from his and stilled a shiver. 'I haven't humiliated myself.'

'Have you not? Were it not for the respect I have for your grandfather, I would have had you forcibly ejected on the first day,' Nik shared in the same conversational tone.

That dark, deep drawl betrayed no anger, but still a reflexive quiver snaked down Olympia's taut spinal cord. Colour ran up over her cheekbones. She forced her head high, dared a second collision with those stunning eyes, but was now careful to blank them out. 'I have a proposition to put to you.'

'I'm not listening to any proposition,' Nik asserted drily.

But in spite of that cool intonation the atmosphere sizzled. She could feel goosebumps rising on her arms. She forgot to look through him without focusing and registered that those extraordinary eyes of his were now roaming over her with unconcealed derision. And instantly she became aware of her creased suit, the flyaway tendrils of hair that had dropped round her hot face, indeed of how very, very plain she was. In fact, just plain ugly next to him: Beauty and the Beast with a transfer of sexes.

And it was that harsh, long-accepted reality that hardened Olympia and gave her the backbone she had almost lost. Ten years ago it had broken her heart not to have even a smidgen of the beauty that might have attracted Nik to her. Now, that contemptuous look of his only reminded her of the pain he had caused her.

'How can you look me in the face?' Nik growled in sudden disgust.

'Easily…a clean conscience.' She flung her head back, challenging him.

'You're a little whore,' Nik contradicted with purring insolence.

Untouched by an accusation so far removed from the truth, Olympia was, however, quite amazed that he still felt a need to abuse her so long after the event. It struck her as almost hilariously ironic that she appeared to have made a bigger impression on Nik with her apparent infidelity than she had ever contrived to make on him as his fiancée.

As a rueful laugh fell from her lips, his darkly handsome features clenched hard. 'Call me what you like,' she advised with patent indifference. 'But I have genuinely come here with the offer of a business deal.'

'Spyros Manoulis would not employ you as his messenger,' Nikos derided.

'Well…in this particular case, of the three of us, it seems that only I have the indelicacy it requires to make this direct approach,' Olympia informed him in taut and partial apology for what she was about to spring on him. 'Can't you just take your mind off what happened ten years ago and listen to me?'

'No.'

Olympia frowned in honest surprise. 'Why not?'

Nik studied her with blazing golden eyes full of even greater incredulity.

Refusing to be discouraged, Olympia breathed in very deep. 'My grandfather still wants you to take over Manoulis Industries. Now, let's face it…that's all he ever wanted, and all your father ever wanted was to ensure that you *got* it. I was just the connecting link…I wasn't remotely important except as a sort of guarantee of family kinship and mutual trust.'

'What is this nonsense?' Nik demanded with raw distaste.

'I'm stripping matters back to their bones…OK?'

'No, it is not OK. Get out,' Nik said flatly.

'No…no, I am *not* getting out!' Olympia's hands trembled and she clenched them into fierce fists. 'You've had ten years of revenge already—'

'What the hell are you talking about?' he grated.

'If you marry me, I'll sign everything over to you...' Olympia told him shakily.

She really had Nik's attention now. His brilliant eyes rested on her with a quality of stunned stillness she had never seen etched there before.

'Not a proper or normal marriage...just whatever would satisfy my grandfather—and he doesn't give a damn about me either, so he really wouldn't be looking for much!' Olympia pointed out, frantically eager to state her case before Nik emerged from what had to be a rare state of paralysis. 'I'd stay on here in England...all I'd need is an allowance to live on, and in return you'd have the Manoulis empire all to yourself and not even the annoyance or embarrassment of me being around...'

A dark flush of red had now risen to accentuate the prominence of Nik's fabulous cheekbones. He grated something in guttural Greek.

'Nik...try to understand that I'm desperate or I wouldn't be suggesting this. I know you think—'

'How *dare* you approach me with such an offer?' Nik demanded thunderously.

'I—'

Striding forward, Nik Cozakis fastened powerful hands to her slim forearms before she could back away. 'Are you insane?' he questioned rawly. 'You must be out of your mind to come to me like this! How could you think for one moment that I would marry an avaricious, brazen little tramp like you?'

'Think business contract, not marriage.' Although Olympia was shaking like a leaf in his hold, she was determined not to be sidetracked by meaningless personal insults. After all, she didn't give two hoots what he thought of her.

His outraged amber-gold gaze raked her pale oval face. 'A woman who went out to a public car park to lift her skirt for one of my friends like a common prostitute picked up out of the street?'

Not having been prepared for Nik to get quite that graphic, Olympia jerked and lost every scrap of colour. She parted tremulous lips. 'Not that it matters now...but that never happened, Nik.'

He thrust her away from him in unconcealed disgust. 'It was witnessed. That you should offend me with such an offer—'

'Why should it be an offence?' Olympia demanded fiercely. 'If you could just turn your back on the past, you would see that this is exactly what you wanted ten years ago and *more*...because I'm not expecting to be your wife or live with you or interfere with you in any way.'

'Spyros would strike you dead where you stand for this...'

Olympia loosed a shaken laugh. 'Oh, he would cringe at my methods, but not three days ago he told me that the only way I would ever win his forgiveness would be to marry you...so it's not like I have a choice, is it?'

'You made your choice ten years ago in the car park.'

Studying the carpet, Olympia felt drained. She saw the pointlessness of protesting her innocence now when she had failed to do so at the time—when, indeed, silence had been so much a part of her revenge.

Warily, she glanced up again, and noticed in some surprise that his attention was welded to her chest. Lowering her own gaze, she saw that a button had worked loose on her blouse and exposed the full swelling upper curves of her breasts. With unsteady hands, her cheeks hot and flushed, she hastily redid the button. Nik slowly lifted his eyes, inky black spiky lashes low on a glimmer of smouldering gold that entrapped her eyes and burned through her like a blowtorch.

'I just wish I'd had you first...if I'd had you, you wouldn't have been desperate enough to go out to that car park.'

'Don't talk to me like that,' she muttered, seriously disconcerted both by that statement and the offensive manner in which Nik was looking her over.

A hard curve to his wide, sensual mouth, he watched her fumbling efforts to tug her jacket closed over her blouse with derisive amusement. 'I'll talk whatever way I want to you. Did you think you'd cornered the market on forthright speech?'

'No, but—'

Nik flung back his handsome head and laughed outright. 'You thought you could come here and ask me to marry you and get respect?'

'I thought you would respect what I could be worth to you in terms of financial profit,' Olympia framed doggedly.

A tiny muscle jerked tight at the corner of his unsmiling mouth. 'You play with fire and you don't even know it. How desperate are you, Olympia?'

Her knees were wobbling. Something had changed in Nik. She sensed that, but she couldn't see or understand what. The atmosphere was so tense, and yet he was now talking with smooth, calm control, and she couldn't believe that he was still angry. Perhaps he had finally let go of that anger, seeing how irrational it was to still rage about something which had only briefly touched his ego. After all, it wasn't as though he had cared one jot about her as a person.

'My mother's not been well—'

'Oh, not the sob story, *please*,' Nik cut in very drily. 'What sort of idiot do you take me for?'

Olympia's hands curled into tight, defensive fists by her sides. 'Maybe I'm just sick of being poor...what does it matter to you?'

'It doesn't.' Making that confirmation, Nik lounged back with innate poise and grace against the edge of his desk and surveyed her where she hovered tautly in the centre of his office carpet. 'However, one fact I will acknowledge. You have more nerve than any woman I've ever met.'

A little natural colour eased back into Olympia's drawn cheeks.

'You must indeed be desperate to approach *me* with a marriage proposal. I'll think it over,' Nik drawled with soft, silken cool.

The rush of hope she experienced left her light-headed.

'Giftwrapped with the Manoulis empire, you saw *no* reason why I shouldn't consider your proposition?' Nik questioned in smooth addition.

She frowned uncertainly. 'You're a businessman, like my grandfather. You would have nothing to lose by agreement, and so much to gain...'

'So much,' Nik Cozakis savoured, regarding her with veiled eyes that were nonetheless surprisingly intent on her.

But then he wasn't really seeing her, Olympia reckoned. He was thinking of the power he stood to gain. Yet the sizzle of unbearable tension still licked at her senses. Her breath shortened in her throat, her heart-rate speeding up. She collided head-on with his steady gaze and the most disturbing sense of dizziness almost overwhelmed her. It vaguely reminded her of the way she'd used to feel around Nik, electrified in all sorts of deeply embarrassing ways by his mere proximity in the same room. But now she put the reaction down to hunger, stress and sheer mental exhaustion, because she wasn't attracted by him any more. It had only been the initial shock of seeing him again which had discomfited her at the outset of their interview.

'So where do I contact you?' Nik enquired.

She stiffened. Her fierce pride was reasserting itself now. There had been nothing personal in the proposal she had made to him: that had been strictly business. But she really didn't want him to know that she couldn't even afford a telephone line. Indeed, she couldn't bear the idea of him finding out just how deep she had sunk into the poverty trap because that felt like a very personal failure. 'I'll give you a number but it's not my own…you can leave a message for me there.'

'Why the secrecy?'

Olympia ignored the question. After a moment, he extended a notepad and pen to her. She scrawled down the number of the only neighbour she and her mother had become friendly with. Mrs Scott was the middle-aged widow who lived opposite them.

'I'll go now, then…' she said, suddenly awkward again now that she had nothing more to say.

Nik shifted a careless shoulder, signifying his indifference.

And she thought then that he wouldn't *ever* use that phone number. Her own shoulders downcurved. Without another word, she walked out of his big fancy office and closed the door with a quiet snap. Damianos was waiting outside, his broad features stiff and troubled.

'He didn't eat me alive,' Olympia announced with a weak but reassuring smile, for she had always liked the older man.

'He will…' The bodyguard muttered heavily. 'But that's none of my business, Miss Manoulis.'

She reached Reception before her head began to swim and her legs threatened to buckle. She dropped down into a seat and bowed her head, breathing in slow and deep, struggling to get a hold on herself again. It was as if she had used up every resource she possessed. Never had she felt so totally drained. But a minute later she got up, hit the lift button and raised her head high again. She had done what she had to do and she was not about to waste time regretting it.

Before she let herself into the flat she shared with her mother, Olympia called in on Mrs Scott to mention that she might be receiving a phone call. The older woman looked amused when Olympia added with palpable embarrassment that if a call did come, she would be grateful if any message was passed on to her personally, rather than to her mother.

But three days later Nik hadn't called.

*   *   *

Exactly a week after she had stood in Nik's office, Olympia
was on the way back from posting yet another pile of job
applications when she saw Mrs Scott waving to attract her
attention from the other side of the road.

Olympia forced a smile onto her downcurved mouth and
waited at the lights to cross. She had been thinking how easy
it was to fall into the poverty trap and find it all but impossible to climb out again. Did prospective employers just take
one look at her less than impressive address and bin her ap-
plication, writing her off as a no-hoper? It had been ten
months since she had even got as far as an interview for a
permanent job.

'That call came this morning,' Mrs Scott delivered with
lively curiosity in her eyes as Olympia drew level with her.

'What call? *Oh...*' Olympia just froze to the pavement.

'He didn't leave his name. He just asked me to tell you
that he'd see you at eight tonight at his office.'

Olympia tried and failed to swallow, her mind rushing on
from shock to register that she couldn't make any assumption
on the basis of that brief a message. It was more than possible
that Nik Cozakis simply wanted to watch her squirm while
he turned her down flat. 'Thanks,' she said tautly, averting
her eyes.

'Job interview?' the older woman prompted doubtfully.

'Something like that.'

'Shameless as it is of me, I was really hoping it was an
illicit assignation! You could do with a little excitement in
your life, Olympia.'

At that disconcerting statement of opinion, Olympia
looked up in frank surprise.

'I'll sit with your mother tonight. I know she doesn't like
to be on her own after dark,' Mrs Scott completed ruefully.

Excitement, Olympia later thought grimly as she teamed a
long navy skirt with a loose, concealing cardigan jacket. Nik
Cozakis had squashed her girlish dreams flat ten years back.
Oh, it had been exciting to begin with, then agonising to sit

by on the sidelines and appreciate that, never mind her lack of her looks, she was so colourless to someone like him that he simply forgot she existed.

A fiancé who couldn't even be bothered making a pass at her! She studied herself in the wardrobe mirror. She looked sensible. She had *always* looked sensible. Once she had experimented with make-up and clothes and she had been proud of her good skin and clear eyes. After all, who was perfect? Only after that disastrous trip to Greece had Olympia lost every ounce of her confidence...

Every year her mother had sent a Christmas card to her father, Spyros, always enclosing a photograph of Olympia, who had been named for her late grandmother. Her grandfather had not responded but Irini's diligence had ensured that the older man always knew where they were living. Then out of the blue, when Olympia was sixteen, had come the first response—a terse three-line letter informing them of the death of her mother's only sibling, Andreas. The following spring an equally brief letter had arrived inviting Olympia out to Greece to meet her grandfather.

'But he's not asking *you*...' Olympia had protested, deeply hurt on her mother's behalf.

'Perhaps in time that may come.' Irini Manoulis had smiled with quiet reassurance at her angry teenage daughter. 'It is enough that my father should want to meet you. That makes me very happy.'

Olympia really hadn't wanted to go, but she had known how much that invitation meant to her mother. And while Irini Manoulis had often talked about how prosperous a businessman Olympia's grandfather was, Olympia had genuinely not appreciated the kind of lifestyle her mother had once enjoyed until a chauffeur-driven limousine had picked her up at the airport and wafted her out to a magnificent villa on the outskirts of Athens.

On first meeting, Olympia had sensed her grandfather's disappointment with a granddaughter who had only a handful of Greek words in her vocabulary. And although Spyros spoke fluent English he had been a stranger to her, a stiff and disagreeable stranger too, who had sternly asked her not to mention her mother in his presence. Indeed, within hours of arriving at her grandfather's home Olympia had wanted to turn tail and run back home again.

The very next day, Spyros had sent her out shopping with the wife of one of his business acquaintances.

'What a lucky girl you are to have such a generous grand-father!' she had been told.

Olympia had suppressed the sneaking suspicion that her grandfather was ashamed of her appearance. The acquisition of a large and expensive new wardrobe *had* been exciting, even if she hadn't been terribly fussed about the staid quality of those outfits. Nothing above the knee, nothing more than two inches below her throat. It hadn't occurred to Olympia that she was being carefully packaged to create the right impression.

The following day, Spyros had informed her that he had invited some young people to his home for the afternoon, so that she could have the opportunity to make friends her own age. While Olympia had been agonising over what to wear, a light knock had sounded on her bedroom door. A very pretty brunette with enormous brown eyes and a friendly smile had strolled in to introduce herself.

'I'm Katerina Pallas. My aunt took you shopping yesterday.'

Her aunt had seemed a pleasant woman, and Olympia had soon come to think of the other girl as her closest friend. She had been grateful for the sophisticated Katerina's advice on what to wear and how to behave. Katerina had never once so much as hinted that full skirts and swimsuits with horizontal stripes might be less than kind to Olympia's somewhat bountiful curves. For all her seeming pleasantness, Katerina's aunt had contrived to buy Olympia a remarkably *unflattering* wardrobe to wear that summer.

Looking back to those early days in Greece, and recalling how naive and trusting she had been, now chilled Olympia to the marrow. Wolves, who had worn smiles inside of snarls, had surrounded her. When friendship had been offered she had believed it was genuine, and she had accepted everything at face value. She hadn't known that Spyros was planning to make her his heir. She hadn't known that the possibility of her marrying Nik Cozakis had been discussed *long* before she'd even met him...or that others might find that possibility both a threat and a source of jealousy.

A security man let Olympia into the Cozakis building just before eight that evening.

She crossed the echoing empty foyer and entered the lift. After hours, with the lights dimmed, she found the massive office block kind of spooky. It felt strange to walk past the deserted reception desk on the top floor and head straight for Nik's office without any fuss or fanfare.

Her heartbeat feeling as if it was thudding at the foot of her throat, she raised her hand and knocked on the door before reaching for the handle with a not quite steady hand and entering.

Only the desk lamp was burning. The tall windows beyond were filled with a magnificent view of the City skyline at night. A million lights seemed to twinkle and sparkle, disorientating her. Then Nik Cozakis moved out of the shadows and strolled forward into view. His superb silver-grey suit lent him formidable elegance.

'Punctual and polite this evening, I note,' Nik remarked.

A wash of colour stained Olympia's cheeks. The balance of power *had* changed. A week ago she had been strengthened by the power of surprise and her own daring, sufficiently desperate not to care about anything but being heard. But all that was past now. She had come here tonight to hear Nik's answer *and* she had politely knocked on the door. He knew the difference as clearly as she now felt it. The whip-hand was his.

'Would you like a drink?'

Olympia nodded jerkily, suddenly keen for him to be otherwise occupied for a minute while she regained her composure.

A faintly amused look tinged Nik's vibrantly handsome features. 'What would you like?'

'Orange juice…anything.' She heard the tremulous note in her own response and almost winced, her full mouth tightening.

He strolled over to a cabinet, his long stride lithe and graceful. She remembered how clumsy she had once felt around him. Had that been nerves or over-excitement? Right at that moment she was *so* nervous she could feel a faint tremor in her knees. As he bent his well-shaped dark head over the cabinet the interior light gleamed over his blue-black hair and she relived how those springy strands had once felt beneath her palms. Flinching, she tried to drag her thoughts into order, but her attention only strayed to the bold line of his patrician nose, the taut slant of a clean-cut masculine cheekbone and the hard angle of his jaw.

'You were always fond of watching me,' Nik mused lazily as he crossed the carpet to extend a crystal tumbler to her. 'Like a little brown owl. Every time I caught you looking, you would blush like mad and look away.'

Embarrassed by that recollection, which was way too accurate for her to dare to question it, Olympia managed a jerky shrug. 'It was a long time ago.'

Nik sank down on the edge of his desk, his attitude one of total relaxation. He saluted her with his glass. 'You were a class act. I was a hundred per cent positive you were a virgin.'

Suddenly Olympia was feeling uncomfortably warm in her cardigan jacket, and although she wanted to meet his eyes with complete indifference, she was finding that her eyes were unwilling to go anywhere near him. She hadn't known what to expect from Nik tonight, but she definitely *hadn't* expected him to refer with such apparent calm to that long-ago summer.

'So…' Nik trailed the word out in his darkly sensual drawl. 'I have only one question to ask before we get down to business. It's like a trick question, Olympia—'

Confusion was starting to grip her. 'I don't want to hear it, then—'

'But you have to answer it with *real* honesty,' he continued with the same unnerving cool. 'It would not be in your best interests to lie. So don't give me the answer you *think* I want to hear because you might well end up regretting it.'

Her mouth was dry as a bone. She tipped her orange juice to her lips. Her hand was trembling and the rim of the glass rattled against her teeth. The tension was so thick she could taste it. But she couldn't think straight because Nik Cozakis now, tonight, was not behaving remotely as he had done a week earlier.

'That night at the club, you may have seen me with another girl…*Theos*, I hope I'm not embarrassing you with this rather adolescent walk down memory lane,' Nik murmured in a voice dark and smooth as black velvet as Olympia perceptibly jerked in shock at what he had thrown at her without warning.

'Why should you be embarrassing me?' she asked between gritted teeth.

'Then let me plunge right to the heart of the matter that engages my curiosity even now,' Nik continued softly. 'Did you go out to my car with Lukas because you were drunk and distressed by what you *may* have seen, and did he then take advantage of you in that state? *Or…*'

Olympia stared fixedly at the desk lamp, outraged resentment and sheer hatred clawing at her. She wanted to toss the remains of her drink in his arrogant face and then hit him so hard, he wouldn't pick himself up for a month. Ten years on, having been judged and found guilty for a sin she had not committed, why should she admit the agonies that he had put her through that night? Why should she further humiliate herself with that kind of honesty? Where did he get off asking her such questions? He darned well hadn't asked her them at the time! Nor had there been any reference to the possibility that she might have seen him carrying on with another girl!

'Or...*what*?' she prompted in a hissing undertone.

'Or...' Nik responded without the smallest audible hint of discomfiture. 'Did you go out to my car with him either because you thought you could get away with not being seen or *because*—'

'I went out to your car with him because I fancied him like mad!' Olympia suddenly erupted, provoked beyond bearing by his sardonic probing, her sea-jade eyes hot with defiance and loathing.

Dark eyes with a single light of gold held to her flushed and furious face. His outrageously long, lush lashes lowered, leaving only the dark glimmer of his gaze visible.

Her tummy clenched and she trembled, an odd coldness spreading inside her, as she met those dark, dark eyes. She spun away, shocked at the gross lie she had thrown at him, shocked that even ten years on her own desire for revenge could still burst back into being and send her off the edge into an insane response, for at the exact same moment she recalled exactly *why* she had come to Nik's office.

'You're just toying with me for your own amusement!' Olympia flung him an agitated glance of condemnation. 'You're going to say no, of course you're going to say no...I really don't know why I bothered coming here tonight!'

'You were desperate,' Nik reminded her with dulcet cool.

'Well, why don't you just *say* no?' Olympia was beyond all pretence now, and she didn't care that she sounded childish. He was winding her up and making a fool of her. She couldn't wait to get away from him.

Nik rose lithely upright. 'No need to get so rattled, Olympia,' he mocked. 'Why don't you take that baggy cardy off and sit down?'

Her hot face got even hotter. She was boiling alive in her jacket, but she folded her arms.

Nik laughed with a sudden amusement that she found even more unnerving.

'What's so funny?' she demanded sharply.

'You always seemed so quiet. I awarded you all these qualities that you never actually possessed.' His expressive mouth twisted with derision. 'But now I'm seeing the *real* Olympia Manoulis. Hot-tempered, stubborn and reckless to the point of self-destruction.'

'These are hardly normal circumstances. Don't presume to know anything about me...because you don't!' Olympia slung back at him defensively.

'But if you don't take the ugly cardy off, I'm going to rip it off,' Nik spelt out softly.

Olympia backed off a startled step. Only now was it dawning on her that she had never really known Nik Cozakis either. Clashing with brilliant dark eyes, she watched him extend a lean brown hand to receive the jacket, and suddenly it didn't seem worth arguing about any more. Tight-mouthed, she peeled it off and tossed it to him. 'You like throwing your weight around, don't you? I should've remembered that.'

Ignoring that comment, Nik cast the jacket on a nearby chair. 'Now sit down, so that you can hear *my* terms for marriage.'

Her eyes opened very wide and she froze.

'*Né*...yes. What you want is within reach, but you may yet choose not to pay the price.'

'The price...?' Thrown by that smooth acknowledgement that he was seriously considering her proposition, Olympia backed hurriedly down into the armchair closest.

'All good things come at a price...haven't you learnt that yet?' Nik murmured in a voice as smooth and rich as honey.

All of a sudden she couldn't concentrate. Having forgotten to keep Nik out of focus, she collided head-on with amber-gold eyes. It was like being suddenly dropped from a height. Such beautiful lying eyes, she thought helplessly, curling her taut fingers into the fabric of her skirt. A quivering, insidious warmth snaked up between her thighs, making her tense, jerk her lashes down and freeze, no longer under any illusion about what was happening to her. As she felt her breasts stir and swell, their soft peaks pinch into straining sensitivity, she was aghast. A tidal wave of embarrassment surged up over her. Already her heart was banging as if she had run a race.

'Olympia...?'

She crossed her arms and lifted her head again with pronounced reluctance. Nik was over by the window at a comfortable distance. He was planning to agree; he was going to marry her. She was home and dry, she reminded herself. What did it matter if her stupid body still reacted to him? He was really gorgeous, really, really gorgeous. It was a chemical response, nothing more. So she didn't like it, in fact she hated that out-of-control feeling, but it wasn't as if she would be seeing much of him in the future.

'You're in shock...I'm surprised,' Nik admitted. 'You seemed so confident last week that you could win my agreement.'

'You weren't very encouraging,' she pointed out unevenly, no longer looking anywhere near him. It might just be a chemical response but she didn't want to encourage it.

'I thought your proposition over at length. I feel I should warn you that I tend to be ruthless when I negotiate...'

'Tell me something I didn't expect.'

'I have certain conditions you would have to agree to. And there is no room for negotiation at all,' Nik imparted gently.

'Just tell me what you want,' Olympia urged.

'You sign a pre-nuptial contract—'

'Of course.'

'You sign over everything to me on our wedding day—'

'Apart from a small—'

'*Everything,*' Nik slotted in immovably. 'I'll give you an allowance.'

She glanced up in surprise and dismay. 'But that's not—'

'You'll just have to trust me.'

'I want to buy a house for my mother.'

'Naturally I will not see your mother suffer in any way. If you marry me, I promise you that she will live in comfort for the rest of her life,' Nik asserted. 'I will regard her as I would regard a member of my own family and I will treat her accordingly.'

It was a more than generous offer, and she was impressed and pleased that there was no lack of respect in the manner in which he referred to her mother.

'Your grandfather was born seventy-four years ago,' Nik pointed out, as if he could see what she was thinking. 'He's from a very different generation. Your birth outside the bonds of marriage was a source of enormous shame and grief to him.'

Fierce loyalty to her mother stiffened Olympia. 'I know that, but—'

'No, you *don't* know it, or even begin to understand it,' Nik incised with sudden grimness. 'Your mother brought you up to be British. She made no attempt to teach you what it was to be Greek. She stayed well away from the Greek community here in London. I am not judging her for that, but don't tell me that you understand our culture because you do not.'

Lips compressed, Olympia cloaked her unimpressed gaze.

'Greek men have always set great value on a woman's virtue—'

'We're getting off the subject,' Olympia said in curt interruption, tensing at the recollection of the names he had called her. In retrospect, she recognised that she now felt sensitive to his low opinion of her morals, and she wondered why on earth that should be.

Just as quickly, she marvelled at her stupidity in allowing him to demand, unchallenged, that she sign away any claim on the Manoulis empire and trustingly depend on his generosity. 'What you said about me signing away *everything*—'

'Non-negotiable,' Nik interrupted with gleaming dark eyes. 'Take it or leave it.'

Olympia breathed in deep. 'I don't care about the money—'

'If you don't care, why are you arguing?'

She didn't trust him. But she did nonetheless trust the promise he had made about her mother, and that was all that mattered, she reminded herself. After all, she would be living with her mother and looking after her. Why *had* she argued?

Nik shot her a sardonic appraisal. 'Do you think I would keep my wife in penury?'

She flushed. 'No.'

He glanced down at the slim gold watch on his wrist and then back at her. 'This is progressing very slowly, Olympia. May I move on?'

She nodded.

'Your belief that we could marry and separate immediately after the ceremony is ridiculous. Your grandfather would not accept a charade of that nature, and nor would I be prepared to deceive him in that way.'

She tensed. 'So what are you suggesting?'

'You will have to live in one of my homes...for a while, at least.'

She focused her mind on her mother's needs and gave him another reluctant nod.

'You give me a son and heir.'

Olympia blinked, lips falling slightly apart.

'Yes, you did hear that.' Nik surveyed her shocked face with cynical cool. 'I need a son and heir, and if I have to marry you, I might as well make the most of the opportunity.'

'You've got to be joking!' Olympia gasped, so taken aback by that calm announcement she could barely vocalise.

Nik elevated a black brow. 'The son and heir is also non-negotiable. And, unless I change my mind at some future date, a daughter will not be an acceptable substitute, Sorry if that sounds sexist, but there are still a lot of daughters out there who do *not* want to be leaders in industry!'

Olympia sat in the armchair staring at him as if he had taken leave of his wits. 'You hate me, you can't possibly *w-want* to—'

'Wouldn't faze me in the slightest, Olympia. You may be damaged goods, but I'm not over-sensitive when it comes to practicality,' Nik delivered, running slumbrous dark eyes over her as if he was already stripping off her clothes piece by piece. 'And as I have no respect for you whatsoever, conceiving a child should be fun.'

'You'd have to make me!' Olympia breathed in growing outrage.

Nik winced and regarded her with semi-screened eyes. 'Oh, I don't think so...I think you'll cling and beg me to stay with you like all my other women do. I'm a hell of a good lay, believe me. You'll enjoy yourself.'

Olympia jerked up out of her chair, so shattered by that speech she was at screaming point. 'You invited me here to try and humiliate me—'

'Trying doesn't come into it. Sit down, Olympia, because I haven't finished yet.'

Olympia threw him a look of fierce disgust. 'Get lost!'

She stalked over to the chair where he had tossed her jacket and snatched it up.

'If I were you, I wouldn't push me,' Nik drawled in a soft undertone that danced down her rigid spine like a gypsy's curse. 'I've got you where I want you.'

'No way!' she launched at him, in such a temper that if he had come any closer she would have swung a fist at him with pleasure.

'Does your mother know about the sordid little encounter

in the car park that concluded your visit to Greece ten years ago?'

Olympia's feet welded to the carpet. Her face drained of colour as if he had pulled a switch. So appalled was she by that question she just stared into space, her stomach knotting with instant nausea.

'Lesson one, Olympia,' Nik murmured with soft, sibilant clarity. 'When I say I've got you where I want you...*listen*!'

CHAPTER THREE

Nik Cozakis strolled across his enormous office and gently eased the jacket from Olympia's loosened grasp to cast it aside again.

He closed his hand over hers and guided her back to the armchair. Positioning her in front of it, he gave her a gentle push downward, and her knees bent without her volition. She sank down in slow motion but settled heavily as a stone.

'You wouldn't...you *couldn't* approach my mother...'

Nik hunkered down in front of her with innate athletic grace. Level now with her, he scanned her ashen face and appalled eyes. 'Oh what a dark, dark day it was for you when you walked into my office, Olympia...' he murmured with silken satisfaction.

Olympia was now in so much shock she was shaking. 'You don't know what my mother knows—'

'What do you think I've spent the last week having done? I've had enquiries made,' Nik told her levelly. 'Your mother was very friendly with your next-door neighbour at your last address, and she was a *very* talkative woman.'

'Mrs Barnes wouldn't remember—I mean, you couldn't possibly...' Olympia was stammering helplessly now, so horrified by the threat he had made she could barely string two coherent thoughts together.

'Unfortunately for you, the lady remembered very well, for the simple reason that your *disappointment* that summer ten years ago has long been an ongoing source of regret to your mother, Irini, and a subject to which she often referred.'

'*No*—'

'You came home to loads of tea and sympathy, you little liar,' Nik framed with slashing scorn, his dark, deep drawl

39

flaming through her like a cutting steel knife. 'You lied your head off about why our engagement was broken!'

Transfixed, Olympia gasped strickenly. 'It wasn't all lies, j-just a few evasions...I mean, I never did what you thought I did in that car park anyway, so why would I mention it?'

Nik shook his arrogant dark head at that claim and sighed, 'You're getting just a little desperate here, and really there's no need.'

'No need? After what you just—?'

'If you do as you're told, you have nothing to be afraid of. I will take your sordid little secret to the grave with me,' Nik promised evenly. 'Hand on my heart, I would really *hate* to be a prime mover in distressing your mother.'

'Then don't!'

Nik vaulted fluidly upright again and spread lean brown hands wide. 'I'm afraid there's a problem there...'

'What problem?' Olympia rushed in to demand jerkily.

'I have a powerful personal need for revenge,' Nik admitted, without a shadow of discomfiture.

'Revenge?' Olympia stressed with incredulity.

'You dishonoured me ten years ago. *Philotimo*...or do you not even know what that word means?' he derided.

Olympia had turned even paler. *Philotimo* could not be translated into one simple English word. It stood for all the attributes that made a man feel like a real man in Greece. His pride, his honesty, his respect for himself and for others.

'I see that your mother educated you to some degree about our culture,' Nik noted. 'I wish to avenge my honour. You shamed me before my family and my friends.'

'Nik...I—'

'I could just about bear you surviving in misery somewhere in the world as long as I never had to see you or think about you,' Nik extended gently. 'Then you came into my office and asked me if I was a man or a mouse and I found out which...just as you're going to find out by the time I'm finished with you.'

'I apologised—'

'But you didn't mean it, Olympia.'

'I mean it *now*!'

Disconcertingly, Nik flung his handsome dark head back and laughed with reluctant appreciation at that qualification.

Olympia took strength from that sign of humanity. 'You're not serious about all this,' she told him urgently. 'You're angry with me and you want to shake me up, and I wish…I really do wish now that I had never come near you.'

Nick dealt her a hard, angry smile. 'I bet you do. Accept that you've brought this particular roof down on yourself!'

Olympia squared her aching shoulders. 'All I did—'

'*All* you did?' Nik rasped with seething force, his lean strong face hard as iron, his fierce anger blazing out at her in a scorching wave of intimidation. 'You dared to believe that you could *buy* me with your dowry!'

Olympia gulped. 'I—'

'Even worse, you dared to suggest that I, Nikos Cozakis, would sink to the level of *cheating* an elderly man whom I respect for the sake of profit. That elderly man is your grand-father…have you no decency whatsoever?' he roared at her in disgust.

Olympia was cringing, devastated by the manner in which he seemed to be twisting everything around and making her sound like a totally horrible person. 'It wasn't like that. I thought—'

'I'm not interested in hearing your thoughts…every time you open your mouth you say something more offensive than you last said. So if you have any wit at all, you'll keep it closed!' Nik advised with savage derision, a dark line of col-our delineating his hard cheekbones. 'You *owe* debts, and through me you will settle those debts.'

'What are you t-talking about?'

'What you *did* ten years ago cost your poor mother any hope of reconciliation with her father. What you *did* ten years ago savaged your grandfather. And what you did to me, you can find out the hard way,' Nik concluded darkly.

Stabbed to the heart by that reminder about her mother, Olympia dropped her head, tears springing to her eyes. 'It wasn't my fault…what happened…I was set up—'

'You're embarrassing me,' Nik slotted in with contempt. 'Lies and fake shame are not going to protect you.'

'You're scaring me…' Olympia condemned tearfully. 'You are really scaring me!'

Nik bent down and closed his hands to hers and tugged her upright. 'You're getting too upset.'

'You can't mean all this stuff you've been saying…'

'I do…but I don't like seeing a woman cry.' Linking his arms round her, Nik stared down at her from his immensely superior height, dark eyes smouldering gold over her damp upturned face.

Olympia's breath tripped in her throat. Suddenly she could feel every individual nerve-ending in her trembling body coming alive. The effect was so immediate it made her head spin. The scent of him was in her nostrils. Warm, husky male with an intrinsic something extra which was somehow exotic and exciting and dizzily familiar. Her heart began to pound in her eardrums.

'Even crocodile tears can get a reaction from me.' Nik slid a big hand down over her hips and eased her so close to the muscular power of his thighs that she gasped, a sort of wild heat whipping over her entire skin surface, leaving every inch terrifyingly sensitive to the contact of his lean, hard physique.

'Nik…no—'

'Nik…*yes*, only you'll learn to say it in Greek and it will be your favourite word,' Nik husked, suddenly hauling her up to him and plunging his mouth down on hers with devouring force.

The hard, sensual shock of him engulfed her in a split second. She had never tasted passion like that before. The stab of his tongue inside the tender interior of her mouth hit her with such electrifying effect her whole body jerked and quivered, a low moan of response breaking deep in her throat. Instantly she was melting, burning, craving more. Her arms closed round him and an amount of hunger that blew her away erupted with the shuddering force of a dam breaking its banks within her.

Nik dragged his mouth free of hers and lowered her to the carpet again, a derision in his raking scrutiny that stabbed her to the heart. 'Hungry, aren't you?'

Devastated by what she had allowed to happen between them, and jolted by a sense of loss so strong it hurt, Olympia swung up her hand to strike him. Nik caught her wrist between firm fingers, the speed of his reaction shocking her. 'Those kinds of games don't excite me,' he warned her drily.

Olympia whirled away from him in a fever of confusion and distress. She couldn't believe that she had responded to him. She didn't want to believe it, any more than she could come to terms with the stormy surge of sexual need which had betrayed her. 'You *wouldn't* tell my mother—'

'Want to run that risk? And destroy the single character trait you have that I can admire?'

'And what's that?' she muttered shakily.

'You love your mother and you don't want her to know what you're really like.'

Olympia felt her jacket being draped round her slumped shoulders. 'You can't want to marry me—'

'Why not? I get the Manoulis empire and a son and heir. Spyros gets a great-grandson—a reward and consolation which he certainly deserves. I also get a wife who really knows how to behave herself, a wife who never, ever questions where I go or what I do because we have a business deal, *not* a marriage,' Nik enumerated lazily. 'A lot of men would envy me. Especially as I didn't even have to go looking for my bridal prize…she put herself on a plate for me.'

'I hate you…' Olympia whispered with real vehemence. 'I'll never marry you…do you hear me?'

'I hope you're not about to go all wimpy on me, Olympia,' Nik sighed. 'I'd find that very boring.'

'You bastard…you rotten bastard…what are you doing?' she demanded as he separated the fingers of her hand.

'Here is your engagement ring… No, *not* the family heir-loom you flung back at me ten years ago…you don't qualify for a compliment like that.'

Olympia stared down mute and stunned at the diamond solitaire now adorning her engagement finger.

'Romantic touch. Your mother will appreciate it even if you can't.'

Nik walked her through a connecting door into another room and straight into a lift.

'You can't do this to me, Nik!' Olympia argued weakly.

'Damianos is waiting in the car park down below. He'll see you get driven home. Get some sleep. I'll see you to-morrow.' As Olympia's cardigan threatened to fall off, Nik wrapped it round her like a blanket. Then he punched the relevant button on the lift control panel for her.

The doors whirred shut. Olympia snatched in a shivering breath, suddenly appreciating that she had a dreadful pound-ing headache and that she had never felt so exhausted in her entire life. She tottered out of the lift into a well-lit basement car park. Damianos glanced at her waxen face and averted his attention again.

Nik's bodyguard had warned her that she would be eaten alive, she recalled dully. She hadn't listened, hadn't believed him, would not have credited in a million years that Nik Cozakis could run rings round her now that she was an adult of twenty-seven. But Nik had run so many rings round her that right now she might as well have been lurching one-legged through a swamp as she followed Damianos to the waiting limousine.

All of a sudden she saw herself as a fisherman, who had dangled a worm as bait and suffered the gut-wrenching shock of a man-eating shark rearing up out of the waves in front of her. And she couldn't believe, didn't believe, flatly refused to even *begin* to believe that Nik would carry through on such threats.

Olympia wakened with a heavy head the next morning.

When she had arrived home the night before, Irini Manoulis had already retired to bed. Olympia had lain awake far into the early hours, engaged in a frantic mental search for an escape. But there was only one possible escape route: she had to have the courage to call Nik's bluff. Why on earth hadn't she mentioned her mother's weak heart? However much he hated and despised Olympia, Nik would not threaten the health of a sick and fragile woman.

Olympia clawed up into a sitting position, using both hands to throw back the heavy mane of hair that rippled in tumbled mahogany waves almost to her waist. She grimaced. A grown woman of her age with hair still *that* long! She remembered her mother brushing it when she was a little girl, but most of all she remembered Nik skimming light fingertips through those glossy strands and saying, 'I love your hair…'

Ten years ago, ferocious bitterness and a mindless need to hit back at Nik Cozakis the only way she could had controlled her. That was why she hadn't defended herself when she'd been accused of betraying Nik with Lukas Theotokas. By then convinced that she had been used and abused by everyone who surrounded her, she had preferred the tag of being shameless to the reality of being exposed as she really was.

Number one wimp and patsy and fool! That was what she had been. She had only been a means to an end to her grandfather, human goods to be traded through marriage to the most prestigious bidder. Nik and his ambitious father had only seen the Manoulis empire, on offer for the price of a wedding ring. Hands had been shaken on the deal before she had even set foot on Greek soil.

And though she didn't want to relive the past, emotional

turmoil had released memories she usually kept buried, and her treacherous subconscious summoned up afresh her first sight of Nikos Cozakis at her grandfather's villa...

Nik by the pool, with a drink in his hand, sleek and designer casual in cream chinos and a black T-shirt. There had been at least ten other young people present that afternoon but Olympia, shy and self-conscious and nervous at being among so many strangers, had seen only Nik.

Nik, laughing at a friend's quip, jaguar eyes glittering in the sunshine. He had stared fixedly at her as she'd emerged from the villa. Deliberate slow cue to double take. Olympia reflected bitterly now on that moment. He had probably looked and thought, She's even plainer than her photographs! But back then Olympia had lacked all such perception, and she had been as transfixed by Nik as an eager new convert before a golden idol.

With a distinct lack of subtlety her grandfather had urged Nik over so that he could immediately introduce them. And Olympia had duly mumbled and stammered and blushed like an idiot, staring a hole in Nik's black T-shirt. Her mind had been a blank while she'd struggled without success to come up with something verbally witty and memorable to hold his attention. But she needn't have worried, Nik had done all the talking for her.

Pained by that memory of her own naivety, Olympia emerged from her reverie and made herself concentrate on the present. The even more hideous present. If she told her mother the *truth* of what had happened that summer, Irini Manoulis would be devastated. Her mother would believe her daughter's version of events, but the humiliation of what Olympia had endured would cause her deep distress. And her gentle parent would never, ever understand why Olympia had failed to hotly defend her own reputation.

But how *could* she have defended herself? Her supposed best friend, Katerina, had backed up Lukas's lying confession of having betrayed Nik with Olympia. Olympia had been sick to the heart, and so bitter after seeing Nik with that beautiful model that all she had cared about was hitting back. Revenge... Yes, Olympia understood both the concept and the craving. Her revenge, her punishment of Nik and her grandfather for misjudging her, had been allowing them to go on believing that she *was* the shameless little tramp they had already decided she was. Nik had been incandescent with stunned rage, his rampant ego severely dented by the shocking discovery that his plain and seemingly adoring fiancée could stray.

Only now did Olympia see how wrong she had been to try to punish them all with their own blind stupidity. Though she could not imagine even now how she could possibly have proved her innocence in the face of the lies that had been told, she knew that her frozen defiance that awful day must have contributed to that guilty verdict. And left Nik fired up with outrage and a desire for retribution that refused to dim even ten years on.

Well, he had given her a blasted good fright the previous evening, Olympia acknowledged. But in the light of day she was too practical, too down to earth to credit that he could have meant all that he had threatened. Giving him a son and heir, for goodness' sake! And what about that extraordinary kiss? The way he had just grabbed her? What point had he been trying to make? That he could kiss her and fantasise about some other infinitely more sexually appealing woman?

Bitterness black as bile consumed her. Of course Nik couldn't be serious...or could he be? He had taken her desperate offer and twisted it into something so threatening her brain had gone into freefall. Having a baby with Nik—worse, going to *bed* with Nik...sheer madness!

In the midst of her feverish thoughts, Olympia glanced at her alarm clock and gasped. Why hadn't her mother woken her up? It was ten to twelve in the morning! Scrambling off the bed, she hurried out of her bedroom and skidded into the lounge, hearing too late the deep burst of masculine laughter that might have forewarned her that her mother had a male visitor.

Lodged one step into the room, clad only in a short faded nightdress, Olympia felt her generous mouth fall open, sea-jade eyes huge at the sight that greeted her. The coffee pot and the best china were out on the dining table. Irini Manoulis was squeezing Nik Cozakis's hand and wiping tears from her eyes. Eyes that were not sad but sparkling, as if an inner light had been relit.

Supremely elegant in a charcoal-grey business suit cut to fit like the proverbial glove, Nik surveyed Olympia with the most supernatural calm she had ever seen. It was as if he was a regular visitor to her shabby home, a lifelong friend of the family, totally at ease with her mother, who was chattering away at speed in Greek, showing more animation than Olympia had witnessed in years.

His dark deepset eyes raked with total cool over Olympia's stricken face. 'Smile, *agape mou*. I'm afraid that when I discovered that you were still in bed I was too impatient to wait any longer to share our good news with your mother.'

'Good...news?' Olympia repeated, like a not very lifelike robot.

Belatedly aware of her daughter's presence, and raising her brows in dismay at the nightdress, Irini Manoulis urged, 'Olympia...go and get dressed! Nik is taking us out to lunch.'

Olympia fell back through her bedroom door like a drunk and dropped down on her bed before her wobbling legs collapsed beneath her. Evidently Nik had come here to tell her mother that they were getting married. Nik was a foe worthy of Machiavelli. And just then, Olympia was fully conscious that she was not Nik's equal in the manipulative stakes.

Barely a step in her wake, her mother entered her room. 'Nik's making the reservations on his portable phone...I need to get changed,' Irini Manoulis shared unsteadily, and then the older woman just flopped down beside her daughter and shook her greying head in an apparent daze. 'Oh, Olympia, I'm in shock...but in such *happy* shock I can't even reproach you for keeping so much from me. What a wonderful young man you are to have as a husband!'

And with that assurance Olympia received a heartfelt hug from her mother, and she sat there like a stalactite in a cave, frozen in time, registering that Nik had bricked up every potential escape route and trapped her with horrific speed and dexterity.

'How long has Nik been here?' Olympia asked weakly.

'All morning...I would have woken you but we had so much to discuss.' Too excited, it seemed, to notice that her daughter appeared to be oddly silent, Irini drew back and clasped Olympia's hands emotively between her own. 'He invited me to live with you, but I said no... When I'm older, who knows? But young couples deserve their privacy, and if I ever return to Greece I would like my father to invite me. For now, London is my home.'

'What...what did Nik tell you?' Olympia studied her mother's workworn hands and gently patted them, struggling to reason, finding it all but impossible.

Irini cleared her throat. 'Everything, Olympia. Indeed he embarrassed me with his honesty, but I can truthfully say now that I have no reservations about you marrying him.'

'Really?'

Her mother sighed. 'I know how terribly hurt you were that night when you saw Nik with that other girl—'

Olympia's teeth ground together.

'You were both too young, Olympia. And the marriage was not to take place until Nik had finished university,' the older woman reminded her. 'A two-year engagement might test even the most decent young man—'

'We'd only been engaged two months,' Olympia heard herself interrupt.

An explosive surge of rage was rising inside her, threatening to choke her to death. How could Nik walk in cold and introduce himself to her trusting mother and contrive to wash himself clean of his past sins? It wasn't fair. It was disgusting, calculating, *horrendous*…

'Yes, but there was alcohol involved. Sometimes when you're young, control is difficult to maintain,' her mother muttered uncomfortably. 'Who knows that better than I? Men have strong appetites…'

Olympia caught her tongue between her teeth before she could blow that dated sexist whopper out of the water.

'Nik had been strictly warned by your grandfather that prior to your marriage there were to be no intimacies between you,' Irini Manoulis pointed out, as if she was telling Olympia something she already knew. 'After what I had done, your grandfather wanted no risk of your marriage having to be brought forward because of a pregnancy.'

In an effort to contain herself, Olympia sucked in oxygen in a long, dragging gasp. The level of Nik's sheer inventiveness hit her like a punch in the stomach.

'It was right to protect you when you were so young.' Her mother sighed. 'But Nik was young too…'

And 'possessed of strong appetites', Olympia repeated, for her own benefit alone.

'Where's your ring?' her over-excited mother was already demanding.

Olympia got up and dug the diamond ring out of the drawer below the wardrobe.

'I told Nik that we had been burgled twice…he doesn't want us to spend one more night here.' Her mother's eyes shone with happy tears as she admired the beautiful diamond. 'It's just like a fairytale…you and Nik. Just like a fairytale, Olympia.'

Ten minutes later Olympia emerged from her bedroom, dressed in black trousers and a loose tunic top. Nik was in the lounge, still using his portable phone, talking in Greek. Olympia studied him, her temper running hot as lava. Just like a fairytale indeed! There would be no going back now.

It would break her poor mother's heart to have her hopes raised so high and then dashed.

'I suppose you think you've been very, very clever,' Olympia condemned as Nik switched off his phone.

He swung round, dark deepset eyes pinning to hers and flaring to gold enquiry, his jawline hardening. Her tummy muscles clenched, her heartbeat quickening. He let his keen gaze roam down the taut length of her, lingering on the thrust of her breasts that even her tunic top couldn't conceal, the swell of her hips, the apex of her thighs, down and down, and then slowly back up again. By that stage Olympia's face was flaming and her teeth were practically chattering with rage. He looked at her as if she was something he already owned, a possession, something he had rights over when he had no rights!

'Irini's happy,' Nik murmured flatly.

'What on earth have you told her about us?'

Nik loosed a soft, sardonic laugh. 'The cover story demanded a shrinking violet afraid to tell her mama that she was again seeing a man whom she had once believed had been less than faithful to her.'

'I will *not* give you a child—'

'You won't get a divorce until you do,' Nik countered, smooth as silk. 'It's your choice.'

Olympia tore her attention from him and covered her furious face with unsteady hands. 'I really *hate* you—'

'Don't muddy the waters with emotions, Olympia. We made a deal—'

'*You* made a deal.'

'To suit my needs...why not?' Nik fenced back with the same unnerving cool. 'Now go back into your bedroom and put on something more festive. This is your mother's day, not yours. You can leave the talking to me, but you need to work on smiling and pretending to be happy.'

'And what if I don't?'

Nik slung her an impatient look. 'You will. You'll pretend for her sake.'

We made a deal. What madness had taken her over that she had imagined they might somehow get married and never live together without anyone even commenting on the fact? What had she been thinking of that first day when she had left her grandfather and came up with that wild idea? What had she imagined she would tell her mother in such circumstances?

'I called Spyros last night,' Nik volunteered. 'He didn't ask a single question, but he said he was pleased and he thought that I would make you an excellent husband.'

'He probably hopes you're going to beat seven bells out of me every night!'

Nik dealt her a sardonically amused glance. 'When we have the mutual pleasure of announcing your first pregnancy, Spyros will appreciate that I was much more sensibly occupied.'

Olympia fled back to her bedroom before she lost her head and screamed at him. For her mother's benefit, she extracted a blue dress and light jacket from her restricted wardrobe and got changed.

Nik took them to the Savoy Hotel. They lunched in state. Just as he had promised, Nik did all the talking. They were to move into his London apartment as soon as possible. Irini would be able to decide where she wanted to live at her leisure. Their wedding was to be held in London in a fortnight. Unfortunately, Nik was far too busy to stay put in London until then, and was in fact flying back to Greece that very evening. Olympia studied her plate at the tone of regret he utilised to make that announcement. He was so clever, she grasped dully. He was ensuring that their supposed relationship was subjected to no closer scrutiny than it had already undergone.

Having escorted the two women back to their flat, Nik

watched his future mother-in-law excuse herself to go and lie down for a while.

'Get Irini to a specialist before the wedding,' Nik advised ruefully. 'I never thought I would say it, but your grandfather is stubborn to the point of cruelty. Surely he cannot be aware of how your mother has been living?'

'He wasn't interested in hearing how we were living...or anything else. Nik, please listen to me...' Olympia pressed her hands together, her sea-jade eyes open and unguarded. 'Feeling as we do about each other, how can we possibly live together?'

'Where did you get the outrageous idea that we were about to do that?' Nik demanded in a dark undertone, lean, strong face hardening. 'Do you honestly think I would want to *live* with a woman like you?'

Utter confusion claimed her. 'I don't understand...'

Nik vented a grim laugh. 'I have some pride. I'll share a bed with you, but I won't share anything else!'

Olympia gazed unseeingly into space. He believed a child could be conceived in mutual hatred? But what did it matter what Nik's plans were now? He might be able to railroad her into marriage on *his* terms but once that marriage existed he would find his mistake. She would not allow him to use her like that. She didn't owe him a child. She didn't owe him anything...

CHAPTER FOUR

ON THE morning of the day that Olympia's wedding was to take place, Spyros Manoulis arrived at Nik's apartment.

Not having heard his arrival, and simply wondering where her mother was, Olympia left the luxurious guest room she had been using swathed in a cotton wrap. She heard the low, tense exchange of Greek and, frowning, peered round the corner into the spacious hall. Her grandfather was standing, his white head bowed and what she could see of his face convulsed with strong emotion, as he gripped both her mother's hands. Instantly Olympia retreated back in the direction she had come.

She was pleased for her mother's sake that some sort of reconciliation was taking place, but Spyros had left it to the very last minute. Olympia was inclined to suspect that only the grotesque prospect of striving to ignore his estranged daughter at his granddaughter's wedding had finally broken down the older man's resistance. Indeed, though feeling intensely critical of *any* person capable of withholding forgiveness for twenty-eight years, Olympia was only humbled by the belated realisation that she had held spite against both her grandfather and Nik for *ten* years already. Her sense of superiority faded fast.

A week earlier she had visited the office of Nik's London lawyer and signed the pre-nuptial contract. She hadn't read it, nor had she sought independent legal advice. As long as her mother's future was secure, Olympia was indifferent to any financial arrangements made for herself. She had got all she wanted already, and she was eager to demonstrate to her bridegroom that she wasn't greedy.

Hopefully, when Nik was brought to appreciate that reality, he would stop being greedy too, and he would see that the outrageous concept of conceiving a son and heir for his own convenience was quite unnecessary when he was still only twenty-nine years old. Having only spoken to Nik on the phone over the past two weeks, Olympia had been steadily recovering the calm and sensible outlook which came most naturally to her. Nik would see sense, of course he would...

'Darling, I'm so sorry...I lost all track of time!' Irini Manoulis entered her daughter's bedroom in a guilty rush and discovered that Olympia had got into her wedding gown all on her own.

Olympia smiled. 'I knew that my grandfather had arrived. I guessed that you would have a lot to talk about...'

In the space of a fortnight her mother had altered almost beyond recognition. She was eating better, sleeping better and, even more crucially, she had recovered her interest in life. True, she was still frail and easily tired, but an existence free of worry and stress was exactly what the heart specialist had advised and now it was hers.

'You look so lovely...no wonder Nik couldn't wait to marry you this time,' Irini sighed fondly.

All brides were lovely, most particularly in their own mother's eyes, Olympia conceded, unimpressed. And Nik was rushing her to the altar because he was eager for the fresh challenge of taking over her grandfather's companies. Hadn't he said so himself when she'd asked him why?

'Nik will restore your confidence in yourself,' Irini said with conviction.

Olympia almost forgot herself and snorted at that unlikelihood. Her wedding dress, purchased along with a modest new wardrobe on the credit cards Nik had had sent to her, *was* beautiful: slender and elegant in shape, with the most exquisite overlay of handmade lace. It was also dazzlingly white in colour, which would undoubtedly curl Nik's lip.

Indeed, Olympia had rejected other gowns purely on the grounds that they were not quite *white* enough.

It did not dawn on Olympia until the last possible moment that her grandfather was intending to accompany her to the church and walk her down the aisle. As she stepped into the limo while Spyros hovered uneasily on the pavement, the atmosphere between them dripped ice.

'I have been too hard on your mother,' the older man conceded curtly as the car drew away from the kerb. 'But I will make up for that now. If Irini wishes to do so, she can make her home with me again.'

'Good,' Olympia muttered grudgingly.

The silence hung.

'You are a very stubborn woman, Olympia. Very like my late and much loved wife—but in that way *alone*,' Spyros hastened to assure her, her supposed lack of morality clearly still so much on his mind he could think of little else even now.

'Thanks...I think.'

'I really do not want to know how you and Nik arrived at this astonishing *rapprochement*—'

'Good,' Olympia slotted in.

'But I feel it my duty to warn you that you may have troublesome in-laws.'

Olympia unfroze and turned. 'Sorry?'

Spyros grimaced. 'Nik's parents are not pleased, but no doubt in time they will come around. I feel sorry for him. They *were* a close family.'

Until he chose to marry the hussy, Olympia filled in, suddenly feeling hugely rejected and bitter. She had liked Nik's parents once, and his lively little brother, Peri, who had been a child of only ten back then.

'Yet they must feel a certain relief at the ending of the other connection...' her grandfather mused, half under his breath.'

'Other connection?'

Spyros frowned, as if she had been eavesdropping. 'I was talking out loud to myself.'

Nik had been having a wild affair with someone even more unsuitable than she was, she decided. Well, what was that to her? Why should she care? He was welcome to his women, who clung and begged. Her chin came up. Olympia could not imagine demeaning herself to that level with any man. But then Nik wasn't the celibate type, as she had discovered to her cost during their brief engagement. She was glad she would be living alone, sleeping alone.

The church was filled with flowers. The scent of them hung heavy on the air. Nik turned from the altar to watch her approach with grave dark eyes, so incredibly handsome he took her breath away. Tall, dark, beautifully built, his spectacular bone structure accentuated by the candlelight. Her heart turned over and skipped a beat. Hadn't she loved him once? Hadn't this once been her dream? How had it all gone so drastically wrong?

Disturbingly, just as they had discussed many years before, it was a traditional Greek wedding ceremony. Nik's godfather played a leading part in the rites, their wedding rings were blessed and then exchanged, and Nik held her hand throughout. Orange blossom crowns were placed solemnly on their heads. They drank from the same goblet of wine. Then they traversed the bible table three times in order to symbolise their promise to preserve their marriage for ever. By the end of it all Olympia was feeling like a real bride and very confused by the sensation.

Emerging from the church into the spring sunshine, and smiling widely for the waiting cameras, she said impulsively, 'I wasn't expecting anything like that...it was a beautiful ceremony.'

'Celebrating one's cultural heritage is fashionable these days,' Nik countered drily. 'Also a good way to personalise the corporate image.'

Olympia stiffened, no longer in any danger of forgetting

the fact that their marriage had more in common with a business merger than a personal event.

'But I believe I'll stop short of the flying of a flag on the roof tonight and having it lowered once I've enjoyed my bride,' Nik completed with dulcet cool.

Her cheeks burning, she turned outraged sea-jade eyes on him. 'You will *not* enjoy me!'

Joining her in the limousine, Nik dealt her a slumbrous look of amusement.

'I *mean* that,' Olympia warned him, staring rigidly out of the tinted windows as the car pulled out onto the road.

A lean hand closed over hers. She yanked her fingers free again. The next moment Nik closed his strong hands round her waist and simply lifted her across the back seat into his strong arms. 'You were saying, Olympia?'

'Let go of me!' she gasped in sincere shock, colliding with smouldering amber-gold eyes as he brought her down on his long hard thighs with shocking ease.

'When I'm ready.' Nik curved long fingers to her chin, bringing her so close she was gazing right into his stunning eyes. 'What beautiful skin you have…'

Her heart thudded against her ribs, her pulses leaping. 'Are we on the way to a reception?'

'Thank you for reminding me…' Dropping his hand to reach for the car phone, without releasing her from the hold of the powerful arm which still enclosed her waist, Nik stabbed a single button with his thumb and spoke with the chauffeur in Greek.

Then he turned his attention back to Olympia.

'Please let me sit on the seat,' she said, in an acidic tone which would have sent a weaker man into cringing retreat.

'You're going to have to work on that sour attitude, Olympia,' Nik censured in husky reproach. 'I don't like it.'

She breathed in very deep. 'Do you think I give a damn what you like?'

Engaged in pointedly surveying the provocative rise and

fall of her full breasts above the lace-edged bodice, Nik slowly lifted his spiky black lashes again, to rest his gaze on her flushed and furious face. 'I'll train you free of charge... after all, I expect to enjoy the results. Now, where were we?' he enquired lazily, his breath fanning her cheek, that dark deep drawl sending tiny little vibrations down her taut spine.

There was a soft snap as something whirred shut. 'What was that?' she muttered, already finding it difficult to concentrate. The atmosphere closed round her again, her throat catching, an extraordinary awareness of her own body taking hold of her.

'Just ensuring our privacy.' His tone was mesmeric as he framed her face with long fingers, letting a thumb intrude between her moistly parted lips. 'You have a very lush mouth, Olympia...'

Focusing helplessly on his golden eyes, a snaking little quiver assailed her. Heat curled low in the pit of her belly, making her push her thighs together to minimise the sudden ache. All her senses were centred on him with fierce intensity. As she recalled the taste and the feel of that wide, sensual mouth, she trembled, raised an involuntary hand and let her fingers slowly slide into his luxuriant black hair, drawing him closer, wanting, *needing*...

He let the tip of his tongue trace the tremulous fullness of her lower lip and she let her heavy head fall back, exposing her throat, jerking with a low gasp of tormented pleasure as he pressed his mouth hotly to the tiny pulse flickering wildly above her collarbone. The urgency inside her was building at an insane rate. She wanted his mouth so badly, and then he let his long fingers expertly explore the curve of her breast through the fitted bodice of her gown and trace the prominent bud of a straining nipple. She moaned out loud, pressing her hand to the back of his, struggling to get air back into her lungs, feeling as if she was on fire.

Nik withdrew his hand and leant back. 'Making love in

cars really does get you going fast...' he conceded lazily. 'Or maybe it's me you're hot for this time... What do you think?'

As that insolent assessment penetrated, Olympia jerked her head up so fast she wrenched her neck, her passion-glazed eyes stricken. For a soundless beat of time Nik studied her with measuring eyes of gold. 'Challenge me and I'm ruthless.'

Olympia dragged herself from him and over to the far corner of the seat, her abandoned body both throbbing and trembling. Perspiration beaded her short upper lip. She was devastated by the power he had over her, devastated by the essential weakness which lay within her. Never one to deny reality, she knew that the fact she had made no attempt to stop him touching her had been as good as encouragement. And that fact filled her with shame.

In the charged silence, Nik loosed a roughened laugh. 'A demonstration that hurt me too, but I'm not planning to consummate our deal in the back seat of a limo.'

Sending the shutters that blanked out the glass division between driver and passenger whirring back, Nik communicated with the chauffeur again. He had toyed with the idea of making love to her, Olympia realised in quivering shock. 'Our deal', not our marriage. *Not* making love either, she adjusted sickly. Having sex would be a better description. And how could she have responded to him as she had? That insane craving for Nik Cozakis knew neither conscience nor pride. It was an overwhelming hunger which had left her pathetically weak in his eyes. And he had just dared to use that weakness to demonstrate how empty her words of defiance could be.

When they arrived at the hotel where their reception was to be held, Olympia was in line for further unpleasant surprises.

In a room set aside for the purpose, Spyros Manoulis awaited their arrival in the company of two lawyers. The dialogue was all in Greek. While Olympia looked on, feeling very uncomfortable, Nik and her grandfather put their signatures to several documents.

The older man took her aside before he left the room and murmured ruefully, 'I want you to know that this was not my choice, Olympia.'

A tide of colour burned her cheeks. She felt intensely humiliated. So even Spyros knew that his granddaughter was to be stripped of any possibility of being personally enriched by her marriage! Mortified by the older man's awareness of that revealing fact, she returned to the table and hurriedly scrawled her signature on the single sheet of paper set out for her. Having assumed that signing away her own rights of inheritance would be a complex matter when so large a business enterprise was involved, she was surprised but relieved that only one document appeared to be required.

But then what did any of it matter? It was foolish of her to be so sensitive, Olympia told herself irritably. She wanted nothing from her grandfather, nothing from Nik either. Nor did she plan to be her husband's beneficiary for one day longer than she could help. How long would it be before Nik tired of their pretence and agreed to a divorce? It wasn't that uncommon for marriages to break up in the very first year, she reasoned, eager to see a light at the end of what promised to be a long dark tunnel. After all, she hated Nik Cozakis, and even in the short term keeping up the charade of being his wife would be a considerable challenge.

Although her grandfather had forewarned her, when Olympia and Nik welcomed their guests she was embarrassed by the chilly reserve of Nik's patrician parents, Achilles and Alexandra Cozakis. They might have attended their son's wedding, but only, it seemed, in preference to publicising their disapproval by staying home.

At first glance she didn't recognise Nik's kid brother, Pericles. At twenty years of age, Peri Cozakis now towered over her. The younger man grinned, brown eyes sparkling with amusement, and only then did a sense of familiarity tug at her.

'Peri...?' she gasped.

'Catch you later...' he teased, well-satisfied by her double take and passing on.

'I wouldn't have known your brother,' she confided to Nik.

'Well, he doesn't *know* you either, except as the good-natured girl who let him slaughter her at basketball...so leave his illusions intact,' Nik responded very drily.

Olympia paled. Dear heaven, she thought in growing dismay and discomfiture, was what had supposedly happened in that wretched car park ten long years ago *never* out of Nik's thoughts for longer than ten seconds? They had been married for little more than an hour and already he had twice made references to that night.

Registering that Nick was speaking to another guest, she lifted her head again, only to freeze. Katerina Pallas stood before her, her hand already extended in greeting but her dark eyes carefully veiled. 'Olympia...'

As she surveyed her one-time best friend, Olympia's own hand simply dropped back to her side again without making contact. The memory of their broken friendship still pained her, and she had never had a friend that close again; betrayed so cruelly, and deeply hurt, she had lost faith in her own sex.

'Perhaps we could talk later...' Katerina suggested with an uncertain smile before she hurriedly moved on.

'How *dare* you?' Nik growled quietly, sending a wave of startled colour into Olympia's cheeks. 'How dare you insult a member of my family?'

Shaken out of her self-absorption by his reaction, Olympia frowned.

Nik dealt her a derisive look. 'I don't care how embarrassed you feel being faced with Katerina again, you will take care to greet her with the respect and civility she deserves!'

'No.'

'What do you mean…*no*?' Nik stared down at her in blunt disbelief.

'I'm not embarrassed and social niceties won't force me into insincerity for Katerina's benefit,' Olympia asserted tautly. 'So keep her away form me. She's just one big fake, and I wouldn't set out to be rude but I *do* have a temper!'

Taken aback by her defiance, Nik drew in a fractured breath, his hard bone structure rigid beneath his golden skin. Only the approach of Spyros Manoulis and the necessity of the bride and groom taking their seats at the top table forced Nik to let that assurance go unchallenged.

Olympia was surprised to register that she felt decidedly smug. Had Nik thought he had married a doormat he could wipe his feet on whenever he liked? Some things—well, plenty of things, Nik would discover he could *not* force. And he wouldn't like that. No, indeed, he wouldn't like that discovery at all. Even when Olympia had been head over heels in love with Nik Cozakis, she had recognised his innate conviction in his own essential male superiority. With blithe ease Nik had simply assumed that he could lay down the law and that she would naturally accept that he knew best in every way and in every situation.

'I really prefer you without make-up,' he had once told her. 'The natural look…'

She had got more subtle, but she had kept on wearing it.

'You're too young to go to clubs, under-age for alcohol as well,' he had reminded her, with an infuriating lack of sympathy. 'Your grandfather wouldn't approve, so you'll have to stay home.'

'I'll got out to a club with Katerina then.'

'You can forget that idea!' Nik had told her instantaneously.

And so they had had their one and only row, hours before the final break-up.

And then, encouraged by Katerina, Olympia had broken in on the boys' night out and what had she found? She tensed, bitter recollection nipping at her. She had found out exactly *why* her fiancé hadn't wanted her around, cramping his style...

After the long meal was over, Olympia was swept onto the floor by Nik to start off the dancing.

'I thought we'd be smashing plates by this stage...tradition and all that,' Olympia heard herself say snidely.

'One more crack of that nature...' His deep dark drawl sizzled above her head.

'And you'll *what*?' she breathed, not liking the sound of her own voice, but in the grip of an uncontrollable need to scratch and draw blood.

'You'll find out.'

'Promises...promises...such a shame you were never very good at *keeping* them!' It was as if Olympia's tongue had developed a life all of its own.

Long lean fingers curved to the nape of her neck, tipping her head back. Smouldering golden eyes blazed down into hers. And Nik caught her up into his arms and took her mouth with a dark, passionate force that went to her head like a drowning surge of alcohol. Taken by surprise, she had no time to put up the smallest defence and the world spun round her at dizzy speed.

The deep thrust of his tongue into her sensitive mouth imitated a far more basic possession. His erotic mastery took her by storm. Her heart-rate rocketed, her pulses leapt, and every inch of her quivering body was engulfed in fiery responsive heat. A need as relentless as it was cruel tore at her with shattering efficiency, leaving her weak and trembling, wholly at the mercy of the physical craving he had unleashed.

As the music came to an end Nik threw back his head and slowly peeled her hands from his shoulders. Brilliant dark eyes scanned her dazed face. 'I like it when you cling, Olympia.'

Gripped by a storm of sheer self-loathing, Olympia forgot that they had an audience and stalked away, only to find escape from the now crowded dance floor blocked by Nik's younger brother.

'It's time I got better acquainted with my new sister,' Peri told her as he folded her lightly into his arms.

'Peri, I...'

The young Greek gazed down at her with surprisingly serious eyes. 'I'm sorry my parents are spoiling your wedding day.'

Utterly taken aback, Olympia looked up at him in real discomfiture.

Peri shook his dark head. 'I can't get over the way they're behaving and I want you to know that I *don't* feel the same way.'

'Thank you,' Olympia muttered awkwardly.

'But I'd be grateful if you'd tell me what's going on...'

'Going on?'

'Come on, Olly,' Peri urged, employing the nickname he had tagged her with as a boy. 'I was a kid ten years ago but I'm not now. Why is my cousin Katerina sidling about looking shifty all of a sudden, and why all this crazy secrecy about what split you and Nik up back then?'

'Secrecy?' Olympia gulped, jolted by that faintly scornful reference to Katerina, not to mention the bald question which had followed. 'Looking shifty' was a remarkably good match of Olympia's opinion of Katerina. She had not enjoyed being forced to watch the other woman put on that convincing show of shy uncertainty in front of Nik.

'I'd also like to know why my parents are embarrassing the hell out of me today. But, more than anything else, I'd like to know *why* Nik is standing back and allowing them to treat you as they have.'

'Maybe your parents just don't approve of my background.' Olympia was desperate to head him off, and belatedly grateful that Nik had forewarned her. Naturally Peri was curious to learn what lay behind so much bad feeling in his own family circle, but she wished he hadn't chosen to open the subject with her.

'They're not out of the ark, Olly,' the younger man reproved. 'My mother wasn't choking back tears all the way through the ceremony just because you were born out of wedlock!'

Olympia compressed her lips, feeling she could have done without that news.

'And considering how she felt about Gisele Bonner being Nik's long-term squeeze, her attitude surprises me even more,' Peri confided, patently unaware that he might be referring to a relationship she had not known about.

Gisele Bonner. The name meant nothing to Olympia, but she somehow knew that she wouldn't forget it again in a hurry. Tilting back her head, she looked up at Peri and said with a cool she was far from feeling, 'You know, Peri…it's really not *that* unusual for parents to be disappointed with their new daughter-in-law.'

'You're stonewalling me,' Peri complained, unimpressed. 'But I warn you. I don't give up easily.'

'And I don't surrender my bride that easily, little brother,' Nik interposed, curving a long arm to Olympia's taut spine and detaching her from the younger man with ease.

Flushed and stiff, Olympia held herself back from Nik as he spun her away from Peri.

'Peri talks a mile a minute…and he's got no discretion,' Nik remarked curtly.

Olympia was aware of his tension but unable to understand its source. If it hadn't seemed such a ridiculous idea she might have wondered what Nik hadn't wanted her to hear. 'He wasn't indiscreet,' she said, and she meant it.

After all, poor Peri was even more out of touch with events than he realised. He didn't know his brother's marriage was a business deal, and a normal bride would have known of any lengthy relationship previously enjoyed by her new husband. Gisele Bonner, Olympia thought helplessly again, her soft, full mouth compressing as she grew rigid as a stick of rock in the circle of Nik's arms. Probably a blonde. Nik liked blondes. Long-legged beautiful blondes, with big blue eyes and not a lot of clothes coverage, she recalled, in her mind's eye recalling the Italian model she had seen him with so many years before.

'Excuse me...' Olympia said flatly, suddenly registering that she was still in desperate need of some breathing space.

Before Nik could guess her intention, she had slid out of his arms yet again and walked off the dance floor to head for the cloakroom. But she only actually got within ten feet of that potential sanctuary before yet another unwelcome event took place.

'Olympia?' Slender and petite in her stylish green suit, Katerina Pallas stepped right into her path.

Shaken, and angered by such a direct approach, Olympia murmured tautly, 'What do you want?'

'We used to be such close friends,' Katerina sighed in a plaintive little-girl voice, looking hurt.

'Save the act for someone who hasn't experienced your idea of friendship,' Olympia advised.

Katerina darted a careful glance around herself, anxious that their conversation should not be overheard. Only then did she risk giving Olympia a mocking smile. 'I almost died of fright when I was invited to your wedding. I thought it might be a trap, but when Nik greeted me just the same as ever I *knew* I was safe!'

'Safe?' Olympia queried.

Katerina tossed her head and laughed. 'It's so obvious that Nik *still* doesn't know what really went on ten years ago.'

'Is it really?' Although Olympia was struggling to look unconcerned, she was mortified by having that reality flung in her face.

But Katerina was too clever to be fooled. If Nik *had* been aware of the appalling lies his cousin had once told, he would naturally have confronted her.

'All hell would have broken loose if Nik had known that I fibbed about you and poor old Lukas!' Katerina gave a little mock shiver of apprehension, her dark eyes scornful as she sneered. 'So, if Nik's married you without knowing the truth, he can only have done it to get Manoulis Industries. You'd still take Nik at any price. Don't you have any pride?'

The knowledge that her lies still stood unchallenged had not only filled Katerina with triumph but had also given her a humiliating insight into the nature of Olympia's marriage. Olympia was cut to the bone.

'More pride than to stand here exchanging insults with you,' she answered tightly, starting to turn away.

But Katerina hadn't finished yet, and she giggled, 'What a come-down for Nik...I expect he'll have to close his eyes and try to pretend you're Gisele Bonner tonight!'

Olympia took refuge in the cloakroom. She felt sick. Her hands were trembling as she rinsed them in cooling water. Katerina hadn't changed one bit. Indeed, it was just a little scary to realise that the passage of ten years hadn't made *any* appreciable difference to the other woman. Katerina was sweet only when she had an audience she wanted to impress, and she still hated Olympia like poison.

However, Olympia did not want a rumour that her marriage was simply a business merger reaching her mother's tender ears. Which it might well do, if Irini Manoulis moved back into her father's home outside Athens. And judging by the way her grandfather was hovering round her mother today, his anxiety for her fragile health writ large in his every protective look and gesture, Olympia reckoned that her parent would not be living in London for much longer.

As she headed in the direction of the top table she saw Nik on the other side of the dance floor. He was scanning the crowds with a frown. Across that distance, brilliant dark eyes suddenly found and held hers. Her heart jumped and her mouth ran dry and she faltered to an unplanned halt. The innate power of that single look electrified her. Involuntarily, she relived the fierce hunger of his mouth on hers and felt the swift answering rise of heat surge at the centre of her trembling body. A wave of burning mortification sent hot colour flying into her cheeks.

No, she hadn't allowed herself to think about that kiss, until just looking at Nik forced her to remember what she would have much rather forgotten. That when Nik touched her, she couldn't yet control her own sexuality. That acknowledgement shamed and embarrassed her. At seventeen she had been able to control and stifle her physical reaction to Nik only because her ability to resist him had never been put to the test. But now the powerful responses she was experiencing frightened and confused Olympia. Nik made her feel like a wanton, and that terrified her. Only frozen indifference would hold Nik Cozakis at bay, and so far she was conscious that she wasn't doing very well in that department.

Nik crossed the floor to her side, black eyes grim. 'It's time for us to leave.'

Olympia tautened. 'But we've only been here a couple of hours—'

'Quite long enough,' Nik cut in with flat finality. 'You put on a lousy bridal act.'

'I don't know what you're talking about...' But even as she said it her memory was serving up taunting images: her silence throughout the meal, the way she had argued with him during that first dance and not once but twice broken free of him to walk away.

'Yes, you do.'

A sensation akin to panic surged up inside Olympia and she dropped her head to study the floor. 'I'm sorry...I'll make a bigger effort.'

'Why tax yourself?' Nik murmured silkily. 'You think I care what people think?'

'I just wasn't concentrating on how I should be behaving. Believe me, I *can* do better,' she asserted in haste, that panicky feeling increasing. All of a sudden the presence of a couple of hundred guests seemed like the best protection she had ever had, and she could not understand why she had been foolish enough to anger Nik by failing to behave like a normal bride.

'Too late. You had your chance and you blew it. Any notion I had of playing the proud bridegroom is long gone,' Nik spelt out very drily. 'So go and say goodbye to your mother.'

'I wanted to spend some time with her—'

'Tough.'

She began to turn away. 'I'll go and get changed first—'

'You'll stay as you are. Your luggage is already on board the helicopter.'

She frowned, taken aback. 'But I have a going-away outfit…I gave my cases to the driver before I left your apartment this morning and told him.'

'I countermanded your instructions,' Nik informed her with complete cool. 'I want to be the one to take you out of that wedding dress.'

Her head flew up, sea-jade eyes sparking. 'But I *told* you—'

'When are you going to learn to listen to what *I* tell *you*?' Eyes black as pitch raked over her and her tummy just flipped at the bleak coldness of that appraisal. 'And I'm not a happy camper right now.'

'H-happy camper?' Olympia stammered weakly.

'Just fifteen minutes ago I watched my cousin Katerina make a second, very generous attempt to reinstate a reasonably civil bond with you,' Nik related with a grim twist of his hard mouth, watching further colour fly into her startled face. 'I also watched her take off again in tears at your rebuff and then pretend that she wasn't feeling well so that she could leave our reception early without causing undue comment!'

Olympia was stunned by that revelation about Katerina. Katerina in tears at her rebuff and making an early departure from their reception? It finally dawned on Olympia that Katerina would still put her in the wrong whenever she got the chance. She was shaken. 'Nik...that's not true. I said nothing—'

'You behaved like a real bitch and I'm ashamed of you. But don't worry about it. I won't be letting you loose socially again,' Nik enunciated with icy clarity.

Olympia, who had never considered herself to be a fanciful woman, felt the most chilling sense of foreboding spread through her, but in angry discomfiture she tried to defend herself. 'Nik, you're not being fair. *She—*'

'I have no interest in hearing your excuses. We're leaving in ten minutes.'

'To go where?'

Belatedly, she recalled the helicopter he had mentioned. 'We're joining my yacht at Southampton. So I suggest you spend those ten minutes with your mother,' Nik incised with ruthless implacability.

Rigid-backed, Olympia approached her parent, who was sitting with her grandfather. Her mother's eyes were troubled. Spyros Manoulis stood up, his beetling brows set in a frown of censure.

'Thankfully your behaviour is now your husband's responsibility, but allow me to tell you that no lady embarrasses her husband in public.'

Olympia's teeth gritted behind her compressed lips. She shot a pained look at her mother, who hurriedly scrambled up to give her daughter a soothing hug. 'Don't let your pride come between you and happiness,' she urged then, in an anxious whisper.

For a dismaying moment Olympia registered that she was attracting censure from every conceivable source, and when that censure also came from the mother she adored, it really hurt. But an apologetic smile softened her mouth, for she was genuinely sorry that anything she had done should have worried the older woman. 'When first we practise to deceive...'

she thought bitterly, for when honesty was forbidden, self-defence was impossible.

Indeed, more than anything else at that moment Olympia felt trapped. Her grandfather thought she was incredibly lucky to have got Nik to the altar, and he would always take Nik's side. Her mother was solely concerned with her daughter's happiness, but Olympia was in no doubt that she had just received a firm scold. Meanwhile, Nik was simmering like a volcano about what he saw as her ungenerous reaction to what he had assumed to be an olive branch from his cousin, Katerina. And, no matter what Olympia did or said, all of them would keep on seeing her as being the one in the wrong.

As Nik came to her side, depriving her of even the ten minutes he had promised, resentment currented through Olympia. Then a sharp and disturbing pang of fear assailed her as she appreciated that the very last thing she could face right now was being *alone* with her new husband.

And wasn't that ironic? she found herself thinking helplessly, as they took leave of all their guests. Ten years ago, the one thing she had most longed for was the chance to be alone with Nik, and the natural privacy offered to a newly married couple would have struck her as a heavenly blessing...

CHAPTER FIVE

AT THE age of seventeen Olympia had fallen for Nik Cozakis like a ton of bricks, and she had hardly believed her good luck at being accepted into the select group of his friends, for she had had nothing in common with them and she had been painfully shy.

Indeed, that summer in Greece she had entered a disturbingly different world. A world peopled with terrifyingly sophisticated teenagers with flash cars and designer wardrobes. And sometimes, looking on, listening to them agonise about their often incredibly superficial concerns, it had seemed to her that though cocooned by so much parental affluence and indulgence, none of them had the slightest idea about what real life was like. But Nik had been the exception. He hadn't *just* been gorgeous. His stunning dark good looks had been matched by an infinitely greater maturity and intelligence.

At the outset of their relationship it had not occurred to her that the regularity with which she'd ended up getting a lift in Nik's car meant anything more than kindness on his part. Then Katerina had told her that Spyros Manoulis had business connections with Nik's father and Olympia had cringed at the idea that her grandfather might have *asked* Nik to look after his English granddaughter.

'You know, I could've copped a lift in someone else's car this time,' she said, on one occasion.

'I don't want to be taking you so much out of your way,' she said on another, squirming with embarrassment when he stayed teetotal all evening at a party and then drove all the way across Athens to take her home. 'Couldn't I just jump on the bus?'

'Please don't feel you have to keep me company. I'm not

lonely. I'm quite happy watching everything that's going on,' she said with determination at a swimming party Lukas Theotokas staged at his home when his parents were abroad.

That night Nik flashed Olympia an incensed look and finally abandoned her to her own devices. Becoming tearful on the discovery that she was not at all happy watching Nik taking her advice and dancing with a very attractive girl, she fled indoors to find a quiet corner where she could break her jealous heart in private.

Lukas found her in the kitchen. 'I see Nik's got another fish to fry tonight,' he remarked, cruelly amused by her reddened eyes and pink nose. 'Someone should have warned you that he likes variety. But I've just had a really good idea…'

Olympia had never warmed to Lukas Theotokas, but she didn't understand why until it was too late; he was one of Nik's closest friends but he was jealous of him. Nik was richer, better-looking and more popular.

'A good idea?' she echoed.

'Why don't you and me have some fun?'

'What sort of fun?' she muttered, genuinely bewildered, for she was well aware that Lukas was crazy about Katerina, who flirted like mad with him but refused to go out with him.

'Yeah…I'd be interested in hearing the answer to that too,' Nik drawled from the doorway several feet away.

Stiffening in surprise, Lukas swung round. Nik said something guttural in Greek and his friend reddened and turned on his heel, leaving Nik and Olympia alone.

'What on earth did you say to him?' Olympia muttered uncomfortably.

'That I'd rip his head off if he said anything like that to you again.' Nik closed one hand over her tightly clenched fingers and drew her to him with cool, controlled determination. And then he kissed her. Lightly, gently and without the passion she had dimly imagined would figure in her very first kiss, but still her tender heart stopped dead for a split second before flying off into orbit.

'You're mine,' Nik sighed, in anything but a lover-like way. 'Don't you know that yet?'

'Yours?' she whispered shakily.

'My girlfriend,' he extended, looking exasperated by her need for that explanatory extension.

Struck dumb, she hovered, lips tingling, shyly studying their linked hands, still unable to meet his eyes. And then the joy hit her so hard she very nearly fell over with the force of it.

'Why do you think I've been running after you?' Nik demanded.

'I thought you were just being nice.'

Nik laughed outright. 'I always have a reason for being...*nice*.'

When she told her grandfather that she was dating Nik, Spyros Manoulis gave her a huge approving smile, and at the time she thought nothing of his lack of surprise. Nor did she smell a rat in the fact that her relationship with Nik stayed low-key and that they were only ever together in a group. On some abstract level she noted her friend Katerina's growing coolness, but she was too much in love and too wrapped up in Nik to pay proper heed.

Since they had only been dating six weeks, she was frankly stunned when Nik asked her to marry him. 'I really care about you...' he confided flatly, not exactly pushing the boat out in the New Age man emotional stakes, staring through the windscreen of his Ferrari as if his life depended on the view. 'I think when we're older we could be great together. You're a really caring person. You like kids and stuff.'

But then what choice had Nik had in that timing? By then she'd been within days of her scheduled return to London. He hadn't said that he loved her, but his marriage proposal had encouraged Olympia to take that belief for granted, and it had also freed her from all reserve. She'd been far too busy

burbling about how passionately and devotedly she adored
and loved him to notice his silence on that point.

Nik had liked that too. In fact, she could still recall him
turning his bronzed classic profile towards her, a scorching
smile slowly forming on his beautiful mouth, all his earlier
tension put to flight. Nik had been relieved that he didn't
have to be more verbal, demonstrative or persuasive. But
Olympia had only been disconcerted when Nik had taken her
home that evening and it had become obvious that Spyros
had known Nik was planning to propose before *she* had.

'Of course I spoke to your grandfather first. He thought
that perhaps you were too young, but I said we'd wait until
I finished university before we got married,' Nik explained
when she taxed him about that.

Indeed the serpent entered Olympia's private Eden only at
the huge fancy party which Spyros Manoulis threw to an-
nounce his granddaughter's engagement.

'I'm just so relieved that Nik's parents like and accept me,'
Olympia admitted to Katerina Pallas.

'And why wouldn't they?' Katerina vented a derisive
laugh. 'I can't think of a single family in this room who
would have said no to an alliance with the Manoulis heiress!'

'What do you mean?'

'Don't you ever get tired of acting like you're the poor
little orphan girl without a blessing to your name? It's getting painful, Olympia,' Katerina said cuttingly. 'Everybody
knows Spyros will be leaving his empire to you!'

The next morning Olympia uneasily broached the astonishing concept of her being an heiress with her grandfather.

'Yes, it's true. Who else do I have?' Spyros was amused
by her unconcealed shock. 'You think I would let you join
the Cozakis family with nothing but the clothes on your
back? You think Nik's father would have been content to see
his oldest son tie himself up *this* young without a little sweetener to the deal?'

'But...but—'

'I'm a self-made man, Olympia. I don't have any illustrious ancestors. The Cozakis family may be top-drawer high-society, but I can match them for every drachma and every tanker they've got!' her grandfather asserted with considerable satisfaction.

'I'm sure you can,' she muttered, thoroughly taken aback by what he was telling her. Suddenly her engagement was acquiring an extra dimension which she had never dreamt existed. A financial dimension...a *deal*?

'I'm proud that I can give you a dowry that puts you on their level. It's a good marriage for *both* families. I need someone to take over Manoulis Industries when I retire, and I can think of no young man who has already shown more promise than Nikos Cozakis. And now, instead of stealing profit from each other by staying in competition,' Spyros continued with positive triumph, 'Nik's father and I will work together.'

That same morning Katerina called in to apologise for her sharpness the night before. She found Olympia in a pensive, troubled mood.

'A dowry, for goodness' sake,' Olympia groaned. 'It's worse than the medieval barter system! Why did nobody mention it to me before now?'

'Women don't tend to get involved in that side of things. But money marries money in our world.' Katerina shrugged her own acceptance of that reality. 'Don't you appreciate how lucky you are? You're not exactly Helen of Troy, but you've still got Nik!'

But would she have got Nik if she had *not* been the Manoulis heiress? That fear powered Olympia's new insecurity. Her trusting assumption that Nik truly cared about her started seeming naive. She began looking to Nik for greater reassurance, but she did not open the subject of her massive dowry with him. She was afraid to confront the possibility of an awful truth. However, day by day that awful truth seeped in on her like a remorseless drowning tide...

Nik did not mention love. Nik did not seem to want to be on his own with her. When she said she'd like to go shopping, he just dumped her on his mother. When Spyros was away overnight on business she asked Nik over for dinner, but he took her out instead, totally ignoring the kind of invitation that most teenage boys could be depended on to take instant advantage of. She remembered all the teasing that had once gone on around Nik, all the earthy references to all the girls he'd supposedly slept with which had once embarrassed her. At one point, becoming desperate to justify his reluctance to so much as put a hand on her breast, she wondered if all that talk had just been fuelled by macho fantasy on his part for his friends' benefit, and if Nik was really still a virgin just like she was!

Indeed, so much did she like that explanation for his remarkable sexual restraint, she actually asked him if he *was* one evening.

'Don't be bloody stupid!' he launched at her in stunned outrage, springing out of his Ferrari as if she had grievously insulted his masculinity, striding up and down with fists clenched with fury before finally bending down to look back in at her with smouldering golden eyes full of sheer bewilderment. 'Where did you get a weird idea like that?'

Scarlet-faced, she mumbled in a mortified whisper, 'I just wondered...I mean, you don't...well, you know...with *me*...and I wondered why not—well...now that we're engaged.'

'We will wait until our wedding night because I respect you as my future wife,' Nik countered flatly. 'If you were Greek, I wouldn't have to tell you that.'

She didn't look at him. For the very first time Nik felt and sounded foreign to her, and he was making her feel like a brazen hussy even while her intelligence told her that she had had the right to ask that question.

'I'm starting to wonder what's going on here,' Nik

breathed harshly. 'Maybe I've been guilty of making false assumptions...are *you* a virgin, Olympia?'

'Yes,' she muttered, angry and confused and embarrassed.

Nik had literally held his breath until he got that confirming response, and she realised then for the very first time that her being a virgin was really, really important to him. And that bothered her. She was only seventeen, but just suppose she hadn't been a virgin? Just suppose she *had* experimented with sex at too young an age? Wouldn't Nik have been able to feel the same way about her? Would he still have asked her to marry him? Suddenly she didn't think so. And it was hard to believe that he could love her and feel like that...

'This is foolish...' Swinging back into the car, Nik reached for her tensely linked hands. 'Very foolish. But you're so shy I wasn't prepared for you to start talking like that, and for a crazy moment it made me suspicious. I just don't want anyone else *ever* to have touched you...'

And it was extraordinary how at that moment, even loving him as she did, and in the midst of struggling to understand his outlook, she felt the most powerful resentment stirring within her. What an idiot she had been to think for one moment that he too might be inexperienced! No, the pure and untouched aspect was to be hers alone! He was denying her what he himself had already enjoyed. He expected her to spend the next two years waiting for their wedding night.

'Suppose...suppose that we wait, and we get married and we find out we don't like each other *that* way?' she suddenly found herself demanding.

Nik withdrew his hand from hers with a jerk. He was disconcerted, not only by her return to the same subject but also by her attempt to argue her point when he had decided that the subject was closed. 'Don't be ridiculous!' he groaned, jaguar eyes golden and derisive. 'Christos...what's got into you today?'

And she might have let the matter drop sooner than risk an argument, but the first incendiary seeds of rebellion were springing up inside Olympia. Nik was defining her limits. She didn't like that. She didn't want to be treated like some untouchable vestal virgin kept in suspended animation until Nik finally told her that, yes, *now* she could have sexual feelings because they were married. He didn't own her. She might love him. But he didn't own her...

Olympia only emerged from her disturbing memories of the past when the helicopter in which she and Nik and Damianos had flown from London began to descend over the water at Southampton.

As the helicopter landed on the helipad on board Nik's yacht, Olympia was stunned by the sheer size of the ship. Indeed, the sleek, futuristic design of *Aurora* left her speechless. Nik had always been very fond of the sea. Yet ten years ago he had not shared that interest with her. In fact he had never once taken her sailing, she recalled wryly. It had been a surprising but telling oversight which Katerina Pallas had remarked on more than once.

About to clamber out of the helicopter, Olympia attempted to untangle her legs from the skirt of her wedding dress while reckoning that no woman had ever been forced to travel in less appropriate attire. Having already sprung out, Nik simply turned and scooped her up into his arms, ignoring her startled squawk to carry her across the deck.

An older man, clad in a smart uniform, greeted them with a wide smile. Quite unfazed, indeed his black eyes gleaming like a conqueror showing off his prize, Nik introduced Olympia to the Greek captain of his crew without putting her down and then strode on. Crossing an area furnished as the most opulent of sun decks, complete with richly upholstered seating and an overhead shading canopy, Nik entered a magnificent large room surrounded by windows on all sides. Olympia, who had naively expected to see little round portholes everywhere she looked, was quite transfixed by the floor-deep stretches of glass and the superb drapes.

'This is the main saloon,' Nik informed her as he lowered her down to stand on the soft deep carpet.

'It's just like a drawing room...' Olympia's annoyance with him was momentarily forgotten as she succumbed to a wide-eyed appraisal of the luxurious furniture, paintings and beautiful flower arrangements.

'*Aurora* was designed to offer all the comforts of home, so that I can work and live on board for long periods.'

Olympia walked over to a window. 'She's enormous... what length is she?'

'Three hundred and eighty-five feet. I'll be glad to give you the official inspection tour tomorrow,' Nik drawled lazily.

Tomorrow, Olympia reflected, her mouth running dry. His raincheck on the timing of any such tour had a significance she was in no hurry to examine. With reluctance, she turned back to face him, shoulders very straight, chin high.

Nik was looking at her. Lush ebony lashes semi-screened his gleaming dark gaze as he let it slowly, sensually roam over her steadily tautening figure. 'You make a beautiful bride, *yineka mou*—'

'Oh, please! Save it for the dummies who cling and beg!' Beneath that earthy all-male visual assessment, a surge of angry pink mantled Olympia's cheeks. She didn't like the way he looked at her; she didn't like it at all. It set every inch of her bristling and filled her with discomfiting heat. But even less did she appreciate the cruel mockery of such compliments. Maybe Nik thought he could *talk* her into bed to make his precious son and heir! No doubt he imagined she would be the same push-over she had been ten years back, still foolish enough to be taken in by his flattering pretence that he found her amazingly attractive!

'I beg your pardon?' Nik countered drily.

'You heard me.' Sea-jade eyes bright as jewels, Olympia stared back at him with a defiance born of growing desperation. Trying to sidestep the issue that this was their wedding night was foolish, she told herself urgently. Once again she needed to make her position clear. Nik was Greek, and bone-deep stubborn. She didn't want him turning up in her bed-room tonight with expectations. The further she allowed his mistaken assumption of supremacy to progress, the tougher it would be to disabuse him of that notion.

'Today you became my wife,' Nik breathed with danger-ous softness.

Olympia clashed head-on with eyes that now smouldered like golden flames. She tried and failed to swallow. It was as if all the oxygen around her had been sucked up by the fire of his anger. She couldn't get air into her lungs. Her knees wobbled together and then locked. 'Yes, but there is no need for me to share a bed with you,' she extended in a breathless rush. 'No reasonable decent need, that is.'

'Very well,' Nik murmured without inflection, his lean, dark, handsome face taut with controlled power, and he turned on his heel to walk away from her.

Released from the terrifyingly intimidating hold of his charged gaze, Olympia slumped as if he had stolen the very backbone from her body. Her head whirled with the on-slaught of sheer dizzy disbelief. *She had won!* For a split second she couldn't credit that reality, but then her common sense took charge to convince her of it. Naturally she had won. Nik was a civilised contemporary male. Sleeping with her and demanding that she give him a child would only have been a vengeful powerplay. All she had needed to do was stand fast and show him that she would not be bulldozed by his forceful personality into doing anything she did not choose to do.

'Are you coming?'

Intoxicated by the sense of triumph filling her, Olympia emerged from her thoughts to notice that Nik had paused to glance back at her in expectant enquiry.

'Oh...' So they were to go somewhere else now, she grasped. The farce of a honeymoon-style trip was no longer required from her. Nik would leave her in some discreet location and no doubt go off sailing instead with one of the clinging, begging little tarts he seemed to require to stoke his rapacious ego. He was going to let them lead the separate lives she had suggested from the outset. A strange hollowness formed inside Olympia at that prospect even as her steps quickened in his wake.

'You won't be able to change your mind again,' Nik delivered as she drew level with him. 'I hope you appreciate that.'

Mr Irresistible, Olympia christened him inwardly, while her face burned with the heat of her offended pride. Nothing like spelling out just how special he thought he was! Did he fondly imagine that she might have secretly craved an excuse to share his bed? Did he think she was one of those dithering women who said no and didn't really mean it? Well, she had got by for twenty-seven years without sex, and where *he* was concerned a hundred years would not be sufficient to change her view of him!

'I know exactly what I'm doing,' Olympia stated with ringing satisfaction.

Nik signalled to the trio of men working in and around the helicopter, where it sat parked about fifty feet away. They all stopped what they were doing. The one she recognised as the pilot approached, and Nik instructed him in Greek. Not quite quickly enough to conceal his surprise, the man dipped his head in agreement, and strode back to the helicopter to issue his own instructions.

'How brave you are...' Nik drawled, smooth as honey.

Inexplicably that tone shimmied down her stiff spine like the spectral hand of foreboding, but Olympia squashed the sensation and lifted her head high.

'You'll be a laughing stock,' Nik remarked with formidable cool.

Frowning in bewilderment, Olympia twisted her head back

round to look at him again. 'What are you talking about? A
laughing stock?'

'If I fly you back to London and dump you back at your
grandfather's feet, many of our wedding guests will be
shocked, but an equal number will simply be amused.'

For an electrified instant Olympia just stared and stared up
into those dark, deepset challenging eyes while her lips
slowly parted company.

'Although I contrived to keep the media away from our
wedding by various stratagems, such an unusual development
will make headlines all round the world. Your mother and
your grandfather will be aghast, but they will also appreciate
that I am quite within my rights to return a bride who refuses
to consummate our marriage.'

Olympia could not credit the evidence of her own ears.
Her wide-eyed stare expanded to take in the hard, clean line
of his sculpted mouth. He had not raised his voice and he
revealed not one atom of anger. He simply spoke as a male
describing an inevitable event.

'You c-can't be serious,' she stammered, in incredulous
denial of the picture such a threat imposed on her. Their
guests would still be partying late into the evening, and as
host, Spyros would naturally remain to the end of the festivities.

'Why shouldn't I be?' Nik enquired with supreme calm.
'You're trying to take me for a fool within hours of our
wedding. We made a deal and you're trying to back out on
it. You picked the wrong guy.'

That assurance rang like a death knell over Olympia. Freedom yawned in the guise of the helicopter now being readied
for take-off again. But freedom at *what* price?

'I wouldn't allow you to humiliate me like that,' she stated
between clenched teeth of fury.

'I would carry you in kicking and screaming—'

'You're out of your mind...it would be medieval to stage

a scene like that in front of our guests!' Olympia countered in outraged condemnation. 'You wouldn't *dare!*'

'What would I have to lose? If you break the terms of our deal, all bets are off for me as well. I'm Greek. I'm better at winning than losing,' Nik shared gently.

A band of tension was tightening like a vice round Olympia's pounding temples. Her imagination, never so active until Nik had come back into her life again, was currently summoning up the barbaric image of Nik delivering her back to her family like a reject while a transfixed and titillated audience looked on. He wouldn't dare, she repeated inwardly, but, meeting the ruthless challenge of his hard dark eyes, she was no longer so sure.

'This is all crazy,' Olympia protested, abandoning fury in favour of a last-ditch appeal for rational, reasonable behaviour. 'So I stay on board this yacht and we pretend everything is normal in our marriage. Who is to know any different?'

'I don't have much time for cheats,' Nik murmured with measured derision.

Olympia paled. 'You're not being fair—'

'When did I say I'd play fair?'

'You *forced* me into agreeing to your terms for this marriage,' she reminded him tautly. 'You blackmailed me by threatening to tell my mother about—'

'I know...' His stunning eyes shimmered, giving him a coolly reflective aspect. 'But count your own sins first. You came to me and you begged me to marry you.'

'I didn't beg!'

'You begged,' Nik repeated drily.

An enormous tide of pain and frustration welled up inside Olympia. 'It doesn't *have* to be like this between us!'

'I like it this way,' Nik contradicted without hesitation, lean, hard-boned face set in implacable lines.

Olympia studied the helicopter, knowing it might as well be a thousand miles out of her reach. Slowly she turned away from that view and moved back into the main saloon. She parted her lips to speak again, and the words she had to say threatened to choke her. 'I'd like to see my room,' she framed woodenly.

Nik pressed a service button. A steward answered the call. Her thoughts in turmoil, Olympia followed in the steward's wake.

Her first impressions of the level of luxury on board *Aurora* were upgraded with every step she took. She saw a gymnasium and a library and a gleaming swimming pool. The state room she was shown into was exquisitely decorated. Two other doors connected with it. Dismissing the steward, she glanced at the gorgeous flower arrangement and the champagne bucket and grimaced.

She checked out the dressing room and was relieved to discover that only her own clothes hung in the wardrobes. At least Nik wasn't expecting to share the room with her! She walked through to the bathroom. Initially awed by the marble fittings, it took her a second or two to notice that there appeared to be something written on the mirror above the double vanity unit.

With a frown she drew closer.

'COMPETE IF YOU CAN!' was printed in crude letters across the highly polished reflective surface.

Compete with *what*? What on earth...?

Her bemused gaze fell on the glossy magazine spread open to one side. A full-page photograph of a gorgeous blonde in a provocative pose met her bemused eyes. 'Gisele Bonner' ran the scribe beneath. Olympia jerked in actual physical shock. Her brain gave her one brief message: wipe the mirror, put the magazine in the bin unread. She ignored the message.

Stomach flipping a sick somersault, Olympia focused on the picture. In a strappy, very short dress that barely covered her behind, never mind much else, Gisele's lithe, golden and perfect body showed to full advantage. She had incredibly long legs, huge baby-blue eyes set above exotically slanted cheekbones, and the sort of mouth cosmetic firms used to sell very expensive lipstick. Her straight strawberry-blonde hair fell like a sheet of polished silk to her elegant bony shoulders.

Olympia backed away from the magazine as if she had been burnt. Don't look, don't read, screeched her brain, but she couldn't control her overwhelming need to know what was written on the opposite page. It was an article on Gisele Bonner, famous catwalk model and long-term 'companion' of Greek tycoon Nik Cozakis. She was thirty-two years old and had sworn that she would never marry because she loved her freedom and couldn't stand children. With a shaking hand, Olympia reached out and turned the page. Faced with a photo of Gisele curved round Nik like a boa constrictor at the Cannes Film Festival, Olympia wished she hadn't bothered.

An audible gasp sounded behind her. Startled, she whirled round. A youthful maid stood in the doorway, her attention welded to what was written on the mirror, her hand flying up to her mouth in apparent dismay. She started to speak in a flood of anxious, apologetic Greek, afraid, it seemed, that she was to receive the blame for that taunting message. Hurrying forward, she swiped at the mirror with a towel, smearing the printed words, rubbing fiercely to clear them from view.

With a soothing but stilted phrase of very basic Greek, Olympia retreated back into the state room. Why did she feel so sick? She could not understand why she felt so sick, so *savaged*! As the maid scurried out, clutching the magazine, Olympia sighed. So Gisele had connections on board *Aurora* Some member of the crew must have been bribed to plant the magazine and the message. Olympia frowned then, as she recalled Katerina's crack about Gisele earlier that day. Was it possible that it could have been Katerina, rather than Gisele, who had wanted to taunt Nik's bride on her wedding night?

Compete if you can! Only what normal flesh and blood

woman would even *try* to compete with a female that gorgeous?

Thankfully, Olympia was not the competitive type. Her tremulous mouth compressed; Nik's former mistress was no business of hers. Refusing to waste any more time wondering who might have been responsible for that petty but nasty message, Olympia sat down jerkily in front of the dressing table. Her head ached from the weight of her hair. With impatient hands she began yanking out the pins which anchored the upswept style she had fixed it in earlier that day. Lifting a silver brush, she straightened out the tangles with a force that left her eyes watering.

Standing up, she reached her hands round her back to unzip her wedding dress.

Halfway out of the garment, she heard the door open. She spun round, words of angry rebuke on her lips at that unannounced entrance. As her gown slithered downward, she arrested its progress by spreading her fingers in a frantic movement. Without it she would have been bare to the waist, for the stiffly boned bodice had made the wearing of a bra superfluous.

Nik was lodged one step inside the door, which still stood ajar behind him.

Her mouth ran dry. Her mind went blank. She just gaped at him.

'I came to ask if you were planning to join me for dinner,' Nik drawled in a curiously hoarse undertone.

CHAPTER SIX

'*DINNER*?' Olympia queried shakily.

'In fifteen minutes...' Nik extended.

His attention was one hundred per cent welded to her. And, involuntarily, Olympia returned the compliment. Nik looked sensational, sleek and elegant as a jungle cat and intrinsically exotic. His black dinner jacket outlined his broad shoulders, well-cut trousers shaping his narrow hips and long powerful thighs with a smooth fidelity of fit that came only with the attention of a master tailor and the richest, smoothest cloth.

Exclusive, sexy, intensely male. She couldn't block him out any more. She couldn't drag her eyes from his lean, dark, devastating face. But then all women noticed Nik, turning their heads for a second lingering glance, often staring. His superb bone structure, level black brows and high cheekbones were matched to a narrow-bridged blade of a nose and a sculpted, sensual mouth that was pure temptation. But it was those molten gold eyes accentuated by the luxuriant fringe of spiky ebony lashes that stopped her heart dead in its tracks.

'Fifteen minutes...' Olympia repeated unevenly, fighting to concentrate as Nik stepped back and shouldered shut the door with a sharp, definitive snap.

A drumbeat of pulsing tension thundered in the atmosphere. As she collided with those burnished eyes, her every skin cell leapt. She could feel each breath quivering through her, the quickening crazy thump of her heart, the swelling mortifying ache of her breasts stirring below the stiff bodice. In desperation, she tore her gaze from his and lowered it.

'But right at this moment eating has to be the last thing on my mind...'

"Sorry?' she mumbled, knees trembling.

In the seething silence, Nik elbowed back his jacket, drawing her attention to a part of him she was not in the habit of studying, and to something that the fine tailoring of his trousers could not possibly conceal. The unmistakable thrust of overt male sexual arousal. And that recognition shocked Olympia rigid and sent a boiling blush rushing up her throat into her cheeks. She dredged her shaken scrutiny from him, expecting to feel disgusted, disconcerted even more when instead a sensation of hot liquid heat snaked up between her clenched thighs.

'*Theos*...you look like a pagan princess,' Nik asserted raggedly.

A pagan *what*? As she lifted her head, she caught a glimpse of herself in the dressing mirror. She stared at that unfamiliar reflection in astonishment. She had forgotten that her hair was loose. Her mahogany mane tumbled to her waist like a waving curtain, one pale naked shoulder displayed, the other concealed, the valley between her breasts accentuated by her folded arms.

'Look at me...' Nik urged thickly.

And she didn't intend to but somehow she did. The growling edge to his accented drawl sent a delicious little tremor running down her taut spine. She flung her head back and looked, encountering scorching golden eyes. She was stunned by the raw desire she saw there.

'Go...' she framed shakily.

'Do you honestly think that I'm about to sit down to dinner in *this* state?' Shifting his broad shoulders in a fluid movement, Nik peeled off his jacket and tossed it aside. Long brown fingers jerked loose the knot on his bow tie, unfastened the top button of his white silk shirt. 'Even you couldn't be that cruel—'

'Me...cruel?' Olympia interrupted in a bewildered daze. Although held by his smouldering gaze like a butterfly pinned to a collector's board, she was hugely aware of the tie dropping to the carpet, the shirt buttons being undone.

'Let the light of reality in here. Ten years back, while you played Miss Prim and Proper Prude and brandished your innocence at every opportunity, I was in absolute *agony*…in the grip of overpowering lust and unable to do anything about it!' Nik's lean, powerful face hardened. 'Did that give you a kick, Olympia?'

'A…a kick?' Eyes huge pools of enquiry, she stared back at him, struggling to absorb his assurance that he *had* found her sexually attractive in those days. That claim ran against everything she had ever believed, and she was paralysed by a sense of sheer disbelief.

'You kept me in a constant state of arousal. I never slept after I was with you. My fantasies about what we were going to do when we got married even embarrassed me!' Nik admitted grimly. 'I wasn't used to going without sex…it was torment; it was seriously painful.'

Olympia just gaped, bereft of all ability to conceal her reactions. 'No…' she whispered in shaken denial. 'No, you couldn't have felt like that—'

'And I don't intend to suffer that way *ever* again,' Nik incised with husky vehemence as he crossed the room and closed his arms round her from behind. 'Because you want me too, *pethi mou*.'

'I don't!' she gasped strickenly.

Lowering his arrogant dark head, Nik pressed his sensual mouth to one pale taut shoulder. A streaking dart of fiery awareness flamed through her treacherous body. 'What's the point of lying about the past now?' he murmured intently.

'I'm not lying!'

Nik progressed with wicked expertise from her taut shoulderblade to a highly sensitive spot just below one small ear. Her legs shook beneath her, her throat extending, her head falling back against his chest.

'I need to hear you admit that you burned for me too, that

only the fear that I wouldn't marry you or that you might lose your precious inheritance held you back,' Nik continued.

As he nipped at her tender flesh with his teeth Olympia shivered violently, and a muffled gasp broke from her parted lips. What he was doing to her put to flight all powers of reasoning. Her skin felt hot and stretched tight over her bones, and she was mesmerised by their reflection in the mirror. Nik with his proud, dark handsome head bent as she leant back against him for support. It was the stuff of a thousand of her secret teenage fantasies. She watched in trembling breathless excitement as he closed his hands to her crossed arms; his skin was so dark against her paler colouring.

'Olympia...' Nik gritted.

She squeezed her eyes tight shut in sudden shame, fighting for control and intelligence. But *still* the wave of unbearable heat and temptation beat at her. She was defenceless. For her, at that instant, there was nothing more important than the feel of Nik's lean, long-fingered hands on her, the hard, muscular strength of him, the sinful imagery flickering behind her eyelids.

'You've got it wrong,' she managed to frame jerkily.

'I've got nothing wrong. Ten years ago you played with me.'

There was no resistance in her as he eased her arms apart. Indeed she could hardly get air into her lungs. Her lashes lifted and she focused helplessly on the mirror again, watched her wedding gown dip to reveal her bare pouting breasts. Shame and excitement fought for precedence inside her. No man had ever seen her like that before, but then that was not a truth she had ever wanted to boast about.

'*Theos*...spectacular,' Nik rasped, with every evidence of sincerity.

Momentarily scientific interest overcame her burning self-consciousness. She watched Nik curve his hands to the full straining mounds which she had always despised. However, no such inhibition afflicted Nik. His frank appreciation of her lush curves was unconcealed. His thumbs rubbed in a skilled caress over her engorged pink nipples.

'Nik…' she whimpered between clenched teeth, the current of fiery response shooting to the very heart of her quivering body to leave her boneless and weak.

'Yes…*Nik*,' he spelt out with curious emphasis.

With a sure hand he eased her gown from her hips and let it shimmy down into a pool round her feet. Her skin warmed as she saw herself fully revealed in the pale silk stockings, blue garter and bikini briefs which her mother had presented her with. No longer could she watch like an onlooker.

'Definitely worth waiting a decade for, *yineka mou*,' Nik pronounced with roughened satisfaction. He lifted her up into his arms and tasted her soft mouth with slow erotic sensuality before he brought her down on the bed. 'Now tell me you don't want me.'

And she couldn't, not with her lips still swollen from his, not with her whole body thrumming as if it had a life of its own, craving more of what he had already given her. 'I can't…' she muttered, shattered by the raw power of what she was feeling in every fibre of her being.

Nik gave her a slashing smile that turned her heart over.

Nothing. She wanted nothing but Nik. In the back of her mind she knew it was a mistake, but that terrible hunger for him, fanned to a white-hot heat by his undeniable desire for her, was infinitely stronger. Nik cast off his shirt to reveal a magnificent hard muscular torso. His skin was the colour of living bronze. Black curls of hair hazed his pectoral muscles, petering down to a silken furrow over his hard, taut stomach. She ran out of breath as he unzipped his trousers. Unlike her, he had not an ounce of inhibition, and he moved with the lithe grace of a natural athlete. She liked watching him; she had always liked watching him. Little brown owl, she recalled painfully. But he was just *so* beautiful…

How could any other man have attracted her after Nik?

Nik had been the ultimate. But Nik had betrayed her, and would surely betray her again, yet still she watched and waited for him, feeling terrifying vulnerable.

'Why have you gone so quiet?' Nik murmured thickly, studying her with hot golden eyes.

Olympia emerged from her increasingly frantic thoughts and her sea-jade eyes widened as she focused on him. He was wearing not a stitch. And all that she had ever been curious about was now on view. She was stunned by the sheer size of him. Her face drenched with colour and she twisted her head away, but the image of him stayed with her, an image both threatening and exciting.

'I could be forgiven for thinking that you've never seen a guy stripped before!' Nik loosed a roughened laugh. 'Or did you find out a long time ago that some men turn on for that little hint of modesty and shyness?'

'That's not funny!' Olympia shot back at him, wounded by his derision and suddenly self-conscious, torn by conflicting needs.

Nik came down beside her and pulled her into his arms. 'I was out of line…but there's something going on here I don't understand. It's spooking me.'

She was more nervous than he had expected, she interpreted, but he wouldn't say that in case she read the comment as another attack. And tears stung her ears, because finally she was facing the fact that she wasn't in control any more. He threw himself back against the pillows, carrying her with him. She was engulfed in him, her breasts crushed by the hard wall of his chest, the hot, musky scent of his skin flaring her nostrils.

'I'm not a bastard in the bedroom,' Nik murmured rawly.

She shivered, the heat of his lean, powerful body percolating through her, the sharp ache of hunger intensifying, 'No?'

'No…so stop shivering,' Nik urged, knotting long fingers

into her hair and tugging her lips hungrily up to the urgent demand of his.

And that kiss was pure naked seduction. He made love to her mouth, dipping his tongue between her readily parted lips to tantalise and torment. Her heart hammered, her tummy clenched and she twisted against him. He shifted in a fluid movement and lowered his dark head to find an achingly sensitive nipple. And she gasped, her back arching against that fierce tug of response she could not withstand.

'I want this to be good for you,' Nik intoned thickly. 'I want to be the best you've ever had.'

And even his dark rich drawl made her quiver. At mind-blowing speed Olympia found herself plunged into a world of sweet sensation, and all the time she was getting hotter and more restive. The feel of his hands on her tender breasts, the knowing expertise of his caressing mouth drove her wild. He traced her feminine mound beneath the thin silk panties and she almost passed out with excitement.

'Please…' she moaned.

Burnished golden eyes held hers then. He said something rough in Greek.

'Nik?' she muttered in a daze.

Lush lashes veiled his gaze. Stripping her of the last barrier between them, his fingers found the damp dark curls at the juncture of her thighs. She twisted and tossed beneath that intimate exploration. The fire inside her was voracious now. She was lost entirely in the hot, teasing torment of Nik's skilled foreplay. She couldn't breathe, couldn't speak, and her body spoke for her, her hips writhing. The need he had taught her to feel had become so powerful it hurt.

Like a lithe dark golden god, Nik came over her and slid between her parted thighs. 'You're so eager…so out of control. Now I finally know how easy it must have been for Lukas to take what should have been mine!'

His tone more than his words made her passion-glazed eyes widen. She gazed up into smouldering golden eyes. Lukas! The name jarred, but she hadn't caught enough of what Nik had said to understand. All that she grasped was that Nik was angry.

'What's wrong?' she gasped.

'Nothing…you're the perfect partner. Hot and willing.'

And, pushing his hands beneath her, he entered her then, in a powerful thrust, and she was so caught up in the newness of sensual invasion she couldn't concentrate. But a split second later she experienced a sharp, jagged pain, and she jerked in dismay under him, a startled cry escaping her.

Nik stilled, pushed himself up and swore in Greek. He studied her with fierce intensity. 'This *can't* be!'

Already the pain was ebbing, allowing her to unlock her tensed muscles.

'You can't be a virgin!' Nik gritted.

Olympia gulped. 'Nik, please…'

Clenching his teeth, Nik groaned with fracturing control, sinking deeper into her, forcing her tender flesh to yield more fully. And the sensation was so unbearably pleasurable that Olympia rose against him with a surprised cry of response. His hungry gaze blazed over her and suddenly he came back down to her again, to drive into her with long powerful strokes. The storm of desire was unleashed again as if it had never been interrupted.

And it was like nothing she had ever imagined. Caught up in the wild primitive rhythm he set, she was overwhelmed by intense excitement. Heart hammering, body burning with the onslaught of that fierce pleasure, she let him push her higher and higher towards the peak she craved with every sobbing gasp she uttered. And when she hit that ecstatic height, wave after wave of shuddering release engulfed her shaken body.

In the aftermath, she was simply stunned. She held Nik close, a crazy kind of joy already beginning to pierce the sense of peaceful satiation. She felt him brush a soft kiss across her brow like a caress. It felt so good to be in his arms, to share in the sort of intimacy she had never known before. Now, at the back of her mind, she was registering that Nik had actually recognised that he had been her first lover. Somehow, at her age, she hadn't expected there to still be any actual physical barrier. So she hadn't thought of that possibility or of what a difference it might make to their relationship. But now it occurred to her that Nik would surely have to accept that she had *not* betrayed him with Lukas ten years earlier.

In an abrupt movement that took her aback, Nik pulled away from her and sprang off the bed. With a frown, she flipped over. He yanked the bottle of champagne out of the ice-bucket and uncorked it, his lean, bronzed profile feverishly flushed and taut.

'Surprise...surprise. And of course you didn't warn me I would be the first. No doubt you imagine that being a virgin...technically speaking...wipes the slate clean!' Nik bit out in a charged undertone as he sent the champagne foaming down into a single goblet.

Noticing that his hand couldn't hold the goblet steady, Olympia sat up, clutching the sheet to her breasts, and simply stared, utterly disconcerted by this renewed attack.

Nik tossed back the champagne as if he was relieving a desperate thirst with water. He snapped the empty glass back on the table and finally looked at her, eyes as black and stormy as a wild wintry night. 'No wonder you were so quiet in bed. Did you think I'd be at your feet crawling and begging for forgiveness now?' he demanded rawly.

'I honestly don't know what you're talking about—'

'Like hell you don't!' Nik was ashen beneath his dark golden skin, his superb cheekbones rigid as he surveyed her. 'This changes nothing. Obviously Katerina interrupted you and Lukas before you could take full advantage of your sordid encounter. But it doesn't make you *innocent*. You still betrayed and dishonoured me...you still behaved like a shameless little whore without an ounce of remorse!'

Olympia was shaken by his reinterpretation of events, and for perhaps the very first time she registered a reality she had been reluctant to confront. 'You really do hate me…' she whispered in sick distress.

'After what you did to me, what did you expect?' As he hauled on his trousers, Nik loosed an unsteady laugh that sent a cold shiver down her spine. 'You covered us all with shame.'

Olympia was now pale as milk, but she still recalled that kiss he had brushed across her brow in the aftermath of their lovemaking, a salutation which to her had signified both tenderness and affection. 'But you…you just made love—'

'You think *that* was making love?' His expressive mouth curled with derision. 'I just consummated our deal, Olympia. You still excite me like mad, but what we shared is called sex. And, as I promised, we both enjoyed the experience, but don't start looking for anything more than that from me!'

Olympia sat there like a statue, not moving a muscle, knowing she couldn't afford to move in case she broke down. And if she broke down she might cry or scream or shout, and he would then know that he had *really* hurt her. Self- preservation kept her still, her face a very pale but smooth oval as she gazed back at him in frozen silence, unable to trust her voice enough to attempt speech.

Nik's penetrating dark scrutiny was one of ferocious intensity. She suspected that he was not getting the reaction he wanted from her and that gave her a bitter comfort. After all, she had sacrificed her pride only to be rewarded with a humiliation that smarted and stung even as her body ached from his intimate possession.

'You look just like you looked the morning after you were caught with Lukas. Cold as bloody charity,' Nik condemned with steadily fracturing cool, a flash of gold now illuminating his stunning eyes. 'You have no loyalty and even fewer principles…that lack in you turns me off most.'

It took every ounce of what little courage she had left, but

Olympia lifted her chin and murmured glacially, 'I hope I conceive this month. I find this kind of scene a complete bore, but interesting for all that. Here you are, twenty-nine years old, and you're still stuck in the past which I left behind years ago, along with other childish things.'

A dark line of blood ran up over Nik's spectacular cheek-bones. He sent her a look of chilling dark fury and she jerked as if she had been struck. 'Be careful how you fight back, *pethi mou*. Too many people have already suffered at your hands. I don't intend to give you a second bite at the same cherry.'

He strode out. She leapt out of bed, raced about gathering up every item of clothing he had left behind and then, yanking open the door, she threw it all out in a heap in the corridor. Then she stood in the centre of the room, naked and shaking like a leaf. Pulling the sheet from the tumbled bed, she hauled it round herself. Next she poured herself a glass of champagne, hoping it would steady her ragged nerves.

But, try as she might, she could not prevent her memories from taking her back to the night which lay at the very heart of Nik's hatred for her. *Hatred*. She shivered and sank back on the bed to recall what had happened earlier that same day ten years earlier...

Katerina had asked Olympia to go shopping with her that morning.

'I just can't believe the way you let Nik boss you around,' Katerina had remarked over coffee in a café. 'Take his plans for his *own* entertainment tonight. If I was engaged to a guy as good-looking and volatile as Nik Cozakis, I wouldn't let him go out to a nightclub without me!'

'I don't want Nik to feel that being engaged means he has to take me everywhere with him—'

'*Everywhere?*' Katerina rolled her eyes in cynical disbelief. 'You already get left behind when he goes sailing. You also got left behind when he flew over to Paris to take care of some business for his father. Why don't we spring
a   sur-

prise on the guys tonight? We could go to the same club and see what they get up to without us.'

Olympia didn't fall for that idea at first. When Nik called in that afternoon, she just asked him up front to let her accompany him that evening. He told her no, she was too young. So she threatened to go out clubbing with Katerina instead.

'No way,' Nik countered. 'Her family wouldn't like it either. We go out in a crowd to clubs. That way we all look after each other.'

'But you've just said that I can't come with you tonight—'

'It's a boys' night...OK?'

And they argued and parted for the first time still angry with each other. Olympia immediately phoned Katerina to take her up on her suggestion that they gatecrash the evening. Katerina made it sound like a really fun thing to do, but by the time the taxi dropped them off at the club Olympia's strongest need was to smooth over the row she had had with Nik.

They found Lukas sitting alone at a table with Nik's car keys lying in front of him. When Olympia asked him in surprise where the other boys were, he muttered something about them having gone on to a party somewhere else.

Olympia had barely sat down when Katerina suddenly gasped, 'Oh, no!'

Olympia looked in the same direction and saw Nik. Lounging back against a pillar, her fiancé was in the act of hauling a beautiful giggling blonde into his arms. Crushing her to his lean, powerful frame, he then fell on her like a sex-starved animal, demonstrating an enthusiasm which he had never let loose in Olympia's radius. It was a process which the luscious blonde openly revelled in.

'Who...wh-what?' Olympia stammered in sick disbelief.

'Ramona. She's an ex-girlfriend, an Italian model...let's get out of here before they see us,' Katerina urged, snatching up Nik's car keys and thrusting them into Olympia's nerveless hands. 'We can talk outside about what to do. You *can't* make a scene in here!'

Hustled away at speed, Olympia was too distraught to protest. But a few feet from the exit Katerina stopped dead. 'Tell me, did you enjoy seeing Nik having a good time for a change?'

Olympia met her friend's glinting dark eyes and blinked, convinced she must have misheard her. 'Sorry?'

'Do you want to know what Nik *really* thinks of you?' Katerina enquired sweetly. 'I can tell you because he told me. He thinks you're fat and stupid and sexless, but worth your weight in gold!'

Olympia's stomach twisted. In deep shock, she stared back at the Greek girl.

'Your grandfather and Nik's father arranged your marriage before you even *arrived* in Athens. Everybody knows that.' Katerina gave her a contemptuous smile. 'Without your future inheritance you're nothing! If Nik needs to console himself with more attractive women, who can blame him?'

Stricken by such malice from the friend she trusted, Olympia whirled away and fled out to the car park. Taking refuge in Nik's Ferrari, as she had been primed to do, she burst into tears. Katerina's words stabbed her to the heart while her memory replayed the agonising image of Nik in an explicit clinch with a female ten times more beautiful than she herself could ever hope to be.

Katerina's spiteful assurances might have been discarded had they not fitted like a horrible blueprint to the flaws Olympia had been afraid to confront in her relationship with Nik. His seemingly instant attraction to her, the speed of their engagement, his sexual restraint which could easily be explained by her own lack of sex appeal. Nik had not only never loved her but had also discussed her and laughed about her with his cousin, Katerina. She felt as if she was dying inside herself, destroyed by her own blind, trusting stupidity.

She must have been sitting there a good twenty minutes

before the driver's door opened without warning. She froze, assuming it was Nik, but it was Lukas who climbed in beside her. 'Didn't want to do this, but here I am anyway,' he groaned, every word slurred by the amount of alcohol he had evidently consumed. 'You're standing on everybody's toes, Olympia. Why did you ever come to Greece?'

'Mind your own business—'

Lukas vented a humourless laugh. 'But it *is*...don't you see? My father says our company will be put *out* of business if your grandfather and Nik's father merge their empires. We won't be able to compete any more. Together, they'll be too powerful.'

'It's not likely to happen now,' Olympia whispered tremulously.

In silence, Lukas let his head loll back against the seat.

And then Katerina reappeared, and approached the car with a triumphant smile on her lips. 'All present and correct, I see. Guess what I plan to tell Nik now...'

'Go away...both of you!' Olympia urged brokenly.

'I'm not finished yet. But you and Nik *are*...I can promise you that. Just in case you were thinking of forgiving him for snogging the face off the blonde, I'm about to go back inside and tell him that I've just caught you and Lukas having a high old time of it here in his car!'

'Sorry,' Lukas framed thickly. 'Filthy set-up, but you didn't leave us much choice.'

'Why would you tell a mad story like that?' Olympia stared at the other girl in total disbelief and got out of the Ferrari to look her straight in the face.

'You're so dumb, Olympia.' Katerina dropped her voice to a level that Lukas could not hear. 'Nik and I were getting really close until you muscled in and pushed me out. *Who* do you think he'll turn to when you're gone?'

It was the last straw for Olympia. No longer in the mood to confront Nik, feeling as gutted as she did, she was desperate just to get away from *all* of them—Nik and Lukas and

Katerina—each of whom had betrayed her. Leaving
Katerina and Lukas in possession of Nik's Ferrari, she took
off across the car park. Unable to face returning to her
grandfather's villa, she ended up walking into a park and
spending what remained of the night on a bench.

And when she finally arrived home, at seven the next
morning, Nik and her grandfather were waiting for her together. All emotion drained from her by then, she clung to
the defensive shell supplied by her battered pride and her
seething bitterness. Indeed, that day she genuinely didn't
care about Katerina's lies or what she herself stood condemned for doing with Lukas if it enraged Nik and outraged Spyros and got her back home to her mother and
London more quickly.

Olympia emerged from her recollection of that ghastly
evening of revelation to find that she had had two glasses
of champagne and that all of a sudden she wasn't feeling
very well. Idiot to drink on an empty stomach! she casti-
gated herself. Why was it that when Nik came into her life
she went haywire and made a total hash of everything?

Normally she was quiet, sensible and reasonably mature.
She didn't fight with people. She didn't make waves. In
the grip of emotional turmoil, Olympia's mind flailed about
in a half a dozen different directions. Things from the past
didn't fit together as neatly any more, she acknowledged,
while wondering why the bed appeared to be lurching beneath her. Was it the effect of the champagne? Standing
up, she watched the carpet ripple with incredulous eyes and
plotted a swerving path into the marble bathroom.

As she ran a bath for herself and got in, she struggled to
concentrate on the shattering confession which Nik had
made. His staggering claim that she, the plain Jane that she
was, had given him sleepless nights of sexual frustration
ten years back. That did *not* make sense—not when she
looked back on their excruciatingly proper engagement,
during

which Nik had behaved as if she'd had a repelling force field surrounding her.

Indeed, she might well have called him a liar this evening had Nik not been demonstrating a most impressive amount of *current* desire for her! Was that why she had lost control and ended up in bed with him? Learning that she could actually *be* attractive to Nik had demolished her defences. Somewhere inside her still lurked the hurt and humiliated teenager who had been forced to see herself as fat and sexless.

Only now, when sanity returned in the aftermath, did she despise herself for surrendering to her own most basic urges, not to mention his. At what price too? 'Consummating their deal'? She shuddered, mortified, tears welling up and running down her cheeks.

Why didn't she *know* more about men? She had spent ten years sitting home with her mother, ten years distrusting the motives of every man who asked her out, and oh, yes, even with her restricted social outlets there *had* been invitations. She had succumbed to a handful of first dates but had invariably seen so many faults in the man she'd then said no to a second date. Yet now she had the horrible suspicion that the only flaw one or two of the nicer men had suffered from had been an inability to be Nik Cozakis! And if that was true, that meant she was a bigger fool than even *he* thought she was!

As she clambered out of the bath a wave of dizziness engulfed Olympia. In the act of wrapping herself in a fleecy towel, she overbalanced and fell. A cry of fright broke from her lips as she hit the floor. She was winded and she was hurt. She lay there sobbing with pain and self-loathing.

'Theos mou!' The first she knew of Nik's arrival was the outburst of Greek, swiftly followed by the domineering command to lie still while a pair of infuriatingly invasive hands roamed over her legs and her arms.

'Haven't you had enough of that yet?' Olympia muttered,

reddened eyes squeezed tight shut while she lay there like a corpse.

'You might have broken something...I heard you scream!'

'Go away!'

'I'm going to make you comfortable here on the floor and have a doctor flown in,' Nik announced, sounding strangely breathless.

'That would be stupid.' Olympia planted both hands on the floor and slowly raised herself. She felt bruised and battered but knew she had done no lasting damage.

Her head was still swimming. She opened her eyes to get her bearings and registered that the bathroom walls were heaving around her. That optical illusion made her feel horribly nauseous.

'Oh...' Nik sighed, suddenly recognising what was really wrong and propelling her in the right direction so that he could offer support while she was ingloriously ill.

He was a true prince when she would have given anything for a male who was squeamish and had simply cut and run to leave her to it. He mopped her brow with a cool cloth, murmured what sounded like concerned things in Greek, and stood by while she freshened up again.

'I'm drunk,' Olympia breathed, rebelling against a sympathy which stung her pride. Glancing up, she collided with liquid dark golden eyes framed by the most astonishingly long dark lashes, and even in the weakened state she was in her heart skipped a beat.

'No, you're seasick,' Nik contradicted without hesitation. 'I should have thought of this, and I'm about to hit the first-aid supplies and make you feel much better.'

He carried her back to the bed, rolled her out of the towel and flipped the duvet over her. The entire manoeuvre was carried out with such dexterity that it was done before she knew what he was about.

'If I had ever got to take you sailing I'd have been better prepared for this,' Nik commented with wry amusement.

'Who stopped you?' she muttered, tongue-in-cheek.

'Spyros,' Nik responded, startling her with that answer. 'Your grandmother *and* your uncle drowned in the sea. Your grandfather didn't trust a teenager to look after you on the water, and with losses like that in the family how could I argue with him?'

As Nik left the state room, Olympia stared into space with shaken eyes. Such a simple explanation for his failure to take her sailing all those years ago, and yet it had never once occurred to her.

Five minutes later Nik reappeared with a glass of water and a tablet. She took them and lay back against the pillows.

Sheathed in tight black jeans and a beige T-shirt, Nik looked younger, more approachable, even more gorgeous than he usually looked. She turned her head away, her pinched profile taut, knowing that she had to look her plainest at that moment.

'I'll be fine now. You can leave me.'

'No. I'll stay until you go to sleep.'

Her lip curled. Nik had been brought up to have wonderful manners. Confronted with apparent female fragility, he went into automatic protective male mode. It meant nothing. It meant no more than the consummation of their marriage *deal*, she conceded grimly. So Nik enjoyed sex. So Nik wanted a son and heir. All she had really learnt was that she didn't need to be beautiful, like his ex-mistress Gisele Bonner, to get Nik in the mood, but since men had the reputation of being less choosy than women were about their sexual partners she was in no danger of seeing herself as irresistible.

'If you wanted me so much ten years ago, why did you never do anything about it?' she whispered suddenly, since he seemed to be in a more approachable mood.

'Get real, Olympia,' Nik urged lazily. 'If your grandfather had found out that we were sleeping together, he'd have sent you home in disgrace. I didn't want to be responsible   for

causing another family rift, nor did I want you thousands
of miles away in London.'

'Yes,' she acknowledged, shutting her eyes.

'Do you want any more good reasons? Like the fact that
a pregnancy would have been a disaster for both of us at
that age? Or the simple truth that I honestly did want to *try*
to wait until we were married?'

Olympia was so disconcerted by the ease with which he
offered those explanations that she said nothing. On yet
another count Katerina had lied. Nik had never found her
unattractive. Indeed, Nik had merely been a remarkably
sensible teenager.

She drifted off to sleep without being aware of it and
wakened in the early hours to the dim glow of a lamp
somewhere close by. When she opened her eyes, she tensed
in dismay to find Nik barely a foot away. Still clothed, he
was lying on top of the duvet in an indolent sprawl, hooded
dark eyes coolly intent on her face.

'What are you thinking about?' she heard herself whisper.

His beautiful mouth twisted. 'Lukas...'

'Magic!' Olympia snapped, and flipped over to present
him with a defensively turned back.

'We grew up together. He was a clown but I was fond
of him,' Nik breathed in a driven undertone. 'When he died,
I felt like I'd let him down.'

'*Died?*' Olympia flipped back over to focus on him with
shocked eyes. 'When did he die?'

'In a drunken car smash a few weeks after you left
Greece.' Nik grimaced as he sat up. 'Apparently he was
rarely seen sober after that night. I don't think he could
cope with what he had done.'

Her face drained of all colour. 'So you're blaming me
for that as well.'

'No, I'm not.'

But she didn't believe him. She felt hollow inside. Lukas
Theotokas had been Katerina's dupe. Had Lukas even appre-

ciated what he was getting involved in that night ten years ago? He had had to get very drunk to play his part in the brunette's plans. It was sad, terribly sad. And if she told Nik now that his one-time friend had deliberately set out to break them up by the nastiest means available, Nik would no doubt go through the roof. She sensed that Nik now saw Lukas as more sinned against than sinning.

'So much grief followed from that night,' Nik stated curtly. 'Katerina failed her exams, and for a while her family were very concerned about her. She was upset about Lukas—'

'I bet she was.'

Nik dealt her a chilling appraisal. 'You think that Katerina should have lied to protect you because you were friends, but for a Greek family loyalty always takes precedence.'

Olympia's face shuttered, bitterness choking her. No longer did she regret her own failure to defend herself against Katerina's lies. What hope would she have had of being believed with a blood relative lying in the role of a witness?

'Katerina lied, and so did Lukas. They both had their reasons, reasons you don't seem to want to find or examine!'

Untouched by that accusation, Nik regarded her with reflective cool. 'There's only one thing which doesn't add up for me—'

'And what's that?'

'No Greek woman would have failed to defend her own reputation. Why didn't you proclaim the fact that you were still a virgin when I confronted you the next day?'

Olympia studied him with incredulous eyes. 'You're kidding me...do you really think I still cared enough about you to demean myself to that level?'

'So you *did* see me in the club with that blonde.'

Twin spots of red mantled her cheekbones as she belatedly realised how much she had revealed with that outburst.

'And you *were* out for revenge when you went with Lukas.'

Infuriated, Olympia began to turn away again, but Nik

forestalled her by closing a strong hand over her forearm.
'So I wanted to satisfy my curiosity. Why not? I have very
little memory of that night.'

'I beg your pardon?'

'Someone spiked my drink. If you saw me with Ramona,
it must have been shortly before I passed out.'

Olympia nodded slowly. 'Mr Innocent…Mr Clean. You
know, my mother may have fallen for that storybook explanation, but I'm a lot less easy to impress!'

Nik's level dark brows drew together in a frown, a disconcerted light in his brilliant dark eyes. 'Are you saying
you don't believe me?'

'Got it in one. Not a nice feeling, is it?' Taking advantage of his loosened grip, Olympia rolled over and stuffed
her face in the pillow.

He swore in guttural Greek.

'Oh, you're so sensitive…' Olympia raised her head to
comment, tongue-in-cheek.

Hard dark eyes struck hers in a raw collision. 'You are
one calculating little witch—'

'There's the door…use it,' Olympia suggested, her furious eyes glittering like jewels.

Instead, Nik knotted his long brown fingers into the
glossy mahogany strands of hair tumbling down onto the
pillow beside him, effectively imprisoning her.

'Nik…wh-what?' she stammered, taken aback.

'Nik, yes—but say it in Greek. *Né*,' he intoned, smouldering dark golden eyes gazing down into hers. He found
her still reddened lips with his mouth and tasted her with
hungry, driving intensity. On a scale of one to ten it was
an eleven-plus kiss. Her head spun; she could think of no
pressing reason why she should breathe if it meant sepa-
rating from Nik for a single second. Her heart hammering,
her pulses racing, she was simply overwhelmed by the explosive excitement channelling through her.

'We don't talk about the past from now on,' Nik instructed

thickly as he ripped off his T-shirt and snaked up his lean hips to unzip his jeans beneath her bemused gaze.

Olympia was utterly disconcerted by a danger she had not foreseen. 'No...we shouldn't...we *can't*,' she stressed, pushing out that more forceful negative, one hand palm down, fingers splayed on the warm, hard muscular wall of his chest. She could feel the steady thump of his heart. Without any prompting from her brain, her fingertips were already flirting with the curling black springy hair hazing his bronzed chest.

'No problem...' Nik murmured silkily, reclining back against the pillows all lithe and dark and dangerous.

She made the mistake of meeting his eyes: a jaguar-gold challenge. Her breath feathered in her dry throat and her breasts tingled, their sensitive peaks pinching into taut little buds. She was shaken to realise that the sort of hunger she had only ever experienced when Nik was actually touching her could now surge through her in a mortifying instantaneous tide even when he *wasn't*.

Like a sleek jungle predator biding his time while an unwary prey circled round him, Nik began to smile. It was the smile of the male who knew exactly what effect he could have on her sex. It was unashamedly primal. Her mind recoiled and urged her to slap him hard, but it was an incredibly sexy smile which made her agonisingly aware of her own femininity.

'I think...' Olympia began tremulously. 'I think...'

'Yes, what do you think, *yineka mou*?' Nik lazily coiled one fine strand of her hair round an indolent forefinger, regarding her with glinting dark eyes semi-screened by spiky black lashes.

Dear heaven, she *wanted* him. The answers came in a flood inside her own head! She wanted to rip his jeans off, she wanted him everywhere at once, she wanted to relive every glorious, greedy minute of the ecstasy he had given her the night before.

'I'm not thinking…I'm not thinking anything right now,' Olympia swore in feverish haste, her cheeks burning.

'I *am*…' Pillowing his tousled dark head back on one elbow with a relaxation that shrieked in comparison with her own frantic tension, Nik watched her steadily with a world of intimate knowledge in his slumbrous gaze. 'Why fight what you're feeling?'

'Is this like your…er…standard seduction routine?' Olympia enquired, struggling to get her mind and her body back under safe lock and key again, failing miserably in an atmosphere so alive with sexual awareness she was trembling.

'At the risk of sounding like a jerk, I've never needed a routine.'

The awful thing was that she believed him, which in turn drew her attention to all the reasons *why* Nik had never needed to go to that much effort. Those stunning dark good looks, that high-voltage sexual aura, the charismatic personality which had been noticeably absent with her in recent times but which she recalled from the past with a deep hurting ache of loss. The teasing, the warmth, the easy smiles…

And suddenly out of that memory came an absolutely unbearable longing to be in Nik's arms again, the kind of sharp, desperate craving which she had no hope of resisting that close to him. She lifted her hand almost clumsily and pushed her fingers slowly, almost fearfully, into his luxuriant black hair, leaning over him awkwardly, her heart banging against her ribs as if she was about to plunge off a cliff.

Nik was gracious. He didn't laugh. He didn't speak. He reached up and drew her down to him and let the tip of his tongue dart and flicker between her parted lips in an erotic invitation that turned her bones to water and made her shiver as if she was in a force ten gale. He set her back from him then, and peeled off his jeans with the sort of loaded, unhurried cool that somehow excited her even more. He kicked back the duvet she was still sheltering beneath and came down beside her with fluid predatory grace.

'I might have asked what you like...' Nik husked in his accented drawl, burnished eyes blazingly intent on her as he spread her out beneath him with a care that sent tormented little ripples of anticipation down her taut spine. 'But you don't know what you like yet, which means we have *so* much to discover together, *yineka mou*.'

Olympia was already boneless, but she was halfway to mindless as well by the time he finished speaking. Breathing took major concentration. Nik teased the corner of her mouth with his own. Unable to bear that teasing, she twisted her eagerly parted lips under his and kissed him with all the untutored eagerness that was flaming through her like an attack force. Fantasy was running riot in her brain. She imagined flattening him to the bed, forcing him to do exactly what she wanted him to do.

'On the other hand, we could race for the finishing line...just this once,' Nik qualified raggedly.

'Please...' was all she said.

CHAPTER SEVEN

WHEN stray sounds penetrated Olympia's slumber, she would have ignored them but for the extra-sensory mental jab that urged her to take heed.

She was so exhausted it took huge will-power just to lift her eyelashes. The curtains were wide, sunlight spilling in. She was tense until she found and focused on Nik. Happiness bubbled up inside her with the force of an unrestrained oil gusher. It didn't strike her as odd that she should be happy. Every time she had stirred in Nik's arms during the night she had experienced that feeling and she had become accustomed to it before she had had the chance or the need to question the sensation.

A stray shard of sunlight gleamed over blue-black hair still wet from the shower, curved like a caress over a powerful shoulder and darted down over the long sweep of Nik's back, gilding his bronzed skin to pure gold. His classic profile was hard, very masculine, until that playful sunshine accentuated black lashes as long and lush as silk fans. And she smiled then, a sleepy, secretive smile, while she watched him haul on his jeans. She just adored those lashes; she always had.

She rolled over to the side of the bed closest to him, lying on her tummy, sleepy face propped on one hand, sea-jade eyes open and unguarded. 'Nik...what time is it?'

'Afternoon. Two o'clock. We haven't eaten since we came on board, nor have we emerged from this state room. I imagine my crew are well satisfied with my virility.'

Olympia didn't really think that dry comment through, merely interrupting on impulse to say shyly, '*I* certainly am!'

Nik stilled. She dropped her eyes, reddened fiercely. Odd how daylight could banish all sense of intimacy, she recog-

113

nised too late. She was annoyed that she had made a comment that would make her mother faint dead away in ladylike disbelief. She had sounded so gauche as well. That final awareness plunged her into an agony of embarrassment.

'It was good,' Nik conceded, without any expression at all.

Good? she almost shrieked back at him in shock. Good? Like a meal, a nice day out, a satisfactory piece of work? Suddenly she was marvelling at the happy contentment she had woken up with only minutes earlier. Had her brain and her memory gone on holiday while she slept?

'But then why shouldn't it have been?' Nik remarked with a slight dismissive shrug. 'I knew we would be sexually compatible.'

Her swollen mouth trembled. She compressed her lips hard. A hollow and sick sense of rejection was swallowing her up like a big black hole. The chill in the air raised gooseflesh on her exposed arms. She had to force herself to look directly at Nik again. She discovered that she needed armour cladding to protect herself from the cool distance in those black eyes, and unfortunately she only had flesh.

Pale and taut now, she muttered, 'I thought we understood each other better now.'

Hadn't there been a closeness which might not have been spelt out in actual words but which had surely been shared, not just in the breathtaking intensity of their lovemaking but in the aftermath too, when he had continued to hold her in his arms?

'Only when we're in the same bed,' Nik delineated with precision.

Olympia felt as if he had slid a knife beneath her ribs and she was fighting not to bleed in front of him. 'I get the message,' she said tightly.

'I'm leaving for a few days,' Nik divulged smoothly, lean, strong features cool as glass. 'Don't ask me when I'll be back. I don't know.'

'I do hope it won't be any time soon,' Olympia told him

sincerely, temper beginning to mount in response to the treatment she was receiving.

Nik froze in his path to the door.

'I'll call you if I'm pregnant. With a little bit of luck you won't have to come back at all!' Olympia added for good measure.

In one accelerated movement Nik swung back. Outraged black eyes lanced into her flushed and furious face.

'However, I should warn you that all that flattering effort you expended on me during the early hours may well prove to have been unsuccessful as it's not really the most promising time of the month for me,' Olympia shared in a tone of bitter satisfaction.

'*Christos*...how can you be so crude?' Nik launched with a flash of white gritted teeth. 'You will not refer to the conception of our child in such offensive terms!'

'Silly me...' Olympia barely recognised herself in the provocative persona which had sprung up inside her own skin. 'I forgot what a feeling and sensitive guy you were. I'm so sorry.'

Nik's big hands coiled into fists. Olympia surveyed that evidence of vulnerability and her heart truly sang a triumphant chorus.

'You are my wife,' Nik growled, not quite levelly.

'No...no...no, I'm not. I'm your partner in this deal, the *sleeping* partner,' Olympia reminded him gently, but her own rage was as fierce as his own. Fury poured through her like petrol ready to ignite, blaze and burn him up, for he had hurt her, he had humiliated her, and he wasn't allowed to do that. No. Not this time. Not ever again.

Nik studied her with smouldering penetration, jaguar-gold eyes rising to the challenge. 'No doubt you would like me to lose control and turn violent. Then you could divorce me and take off to freedom with millions of banknotes...is that what you think?'

Olympia frowned, giving the suggestion serious thought.

Strange how the prospect of freedom, even accompanied by millions of banknotes, failed to tempt her, she conceded worriedly.

'Get down and dirty with good legal counsel,' Nik advised in abrasive continuance. 'As you should have done *before* you signed our marriage contract.'

Completely in the dark as to his meaning, Olympia muttered, 'Sorry?'

'I can be the biggest bastard on the surface of this earth, but if you choose to walk out you leave our children behind and you leave the marriage as poor as you entered it,' Nik informed her with grim satisfaction. 'My lawyers said you'd never sign so punitive a contract. They said you'd throw hysterics when you read the first clause and that by the time you read the final one you'd be in need of resuscitation. But then, they don't know you the way *I* know you.'

Olympia was now hanging on his every word. 'Don't they?'

'All you were thinking about was the money,' Nik completed with derision.

'No...not that,' she muttered.

Nik reached the door.

Her blood ran cold as she recognised the amount of control Nik wanted over her; he was even willing to use any children they might have as a weapon against her. He might be fond of calling their marriage a deal, but it was not a term she should take literally. Nik had no plans to treat her as a partner, even of the junior variety. Nik was more into ownership than partnership.

In genuine shock at that realisation, Olympia whispered shakily, 'How can you still hate me this much?'

Teach me, she was thinking crazily, teach me how to hate as hard and for as long as you have hated. It was a lesson she seemed in dire need of learning.

Nik turned back his arrogant dark head. Black eyes without a single softening shade of liquid gold met hers with a coldness that frightened the life out of her. 'I really loved you once. Or is that too deep and sensitive a connection for you to understand?'

Three days later, Olympia congratulated herself: she wasn't crying any more.

I really loved you once. An admission made with the darkest, deepest and most bitter sincerity. A statement she could not dismiss, protest or doubt. And, not to put too fine a point on it, that confession had slaughtered Olympia where she sat. It had ruined her appetite and destroyed her ability to sleep. It had ripped apart the entire fabric of her view of the past and in so doing had sunk her into deep emotional turmoil.

She slid from the extreme of wanting to kill Nik for telling her ten years too late to the extreme of wanting to kill Nik for telling her and then taking off in his wretched helicopter, leaving neither forwarding address nor phone number. Why had he left her? Where had he gone?

Meanwhile *Aurora* kept on sailing, without ever putting into port. Olympia became acquainted with the gym, the sauna, the swimming pool, the library, the fantastic meals and the level of luxury and personal care now available to her at any hour of the day and night. If she wanted her hair done her maid was a hairdresser, with two dozen styles at her fingertips. If she wanted to listen to music the yacht had two bars, a dance floor and a state-of-the-art sound system. And if she wanted to phone her mother the satellite communications systems could handle anything.

Unfortunately talking to Irini Manoulis entailed skilled diplomacy as Olympia bent over backwards not to actually tell a lie. Yes, she was having a wonderful, stupendous time on her honeymoon. Just one problem—and that she did not choose to share with her mother. She was enjoying it solo.

So Nik had *loved* her. Never mentioned it though, never brought himself to the dangerous brink of saying the words which might have kept them together and encouraged her to fight Katerina's lies. The fiancé who had never held hands with her, who had backed off fast when she threatened to get slushy, who had never given her flowers, cute gifts, cards, anything that might have spoke for him! Nik had been such a cool guy at nineteen. *Except* when he'd proposed…

And she put her head down and wept again, because at twenty-seven, armed with the knowledge of the love she had doubted at seventeen, she found that clumsy, unromantic marriage proposal of Nik's back then especially poignant, especially painful. She remembered his intense relief when she'd just said yes and then proceeded to do all his talking for him.

And now, in the present, she agonised over *why* Nik had left her alone on *Aurora*. After the night they had shared, she hadn't expected that. Maybe getting her to bed had just been a challenge for Nik. Or maybe he had simply got bored with her, bored with the whole set-up. She hadn't been much of a challenge. Nor could she had been an exciting partner for so experienced a lover. What had been so special for her had not necessarily been remotely special for Nik, and she was ashamed of her own naivety. She had been so happy when she'd wakened, but Nik had been stone-cold and remote.

Out of bed, he truly did hate her. Why? Once he had loved her and she had *hurt* him. Forgiving and forgetting wasn't on his agenda. Nik was ready to fight to the last ditch to hang on to his bitter desire for revenge. She had compromised his sense of honour, shamed him in front of others. Too late did she recognise the intensity with which her Greek husband still felt those wounds on his masculinity. What a number Katerina and Lukas had worked on them both that night! Only now did Olympia find that she *could* accept Nik's side of the story. Lukas must have spiked Nik's drink and invited Nik's ex-girlfriend to join them at that club. It was all so far in the past, yet that night was still poisoning the present and causing her unimaginable pain.

Why so much pain? And why was she missing Nik so dreadfully? She ought to have been glad to see him go, grateful that he stayed away. But she wasn't. She was hurting too, shaken that Nik was as bitter if not more bitter than she had been. Her own emotions were all over the place. Either she had never got over Nik or she was falling for him again. And that suspicion made her very angry with herself. Nik had married her to gain the Manoulis empire and Nik would divorce her as soon as she gave him a son and heir. It was a straight business deal that had no room for emotion.

When Nik had been gone for five days, Olympia decided it was time to abandon ship. Given the opportunity to travel, she ought to be taking full advantage of it, not sitting around on board *Aurora* with nothing to do but sunbathe and think about a husband who had dumped her for more exciting things within a day of their wedding.

Nik's captain spoke excellent English, and when Olympia told him that she would like to visit the port of Malaga on the Spanish coast he was happy to be furnished with a destination and even mentioned the necessity of taking on fresh supplies. Evidently Nik had not been in touch since his departure, a state of affairs which was the perfect vehicle for her own intentions.

When the yacht docked at Malaga, as an act of exorcism and a statement of her new independence, Olympia asked her maid to cut twelve inches off her hair; she liked the results. However, the Captain looked dismayed when Olympia appeared, to disembark with a travelling bag in her hand. She told him that she would return in exactly a week and then she hastened towards the gangway like an escaping prisoner. It rather spoiled the moment when the older man intercepted her to point out that there were certain formalities to be observed before she set foot in a country of which she was not a resident.

However, within half an hour Olympia had satisfied those requirements and she was on her way. Having read Washington Irving's *Tales of the Alhambra* the previous year, and renewed her acquaintance with the book during Nik's absence, Olympia had her itinerary all worked out. She was heading for Granada, to see the wonderful gardens and the palace-fortress of the legendary Moorish sultans. She caught the train from Malaga, but when she arrived it was late afternoon. Wanting more than a couple of hours to explore the Alhambra complex, she found a small city *pensione* in which to spend the night.

The next morning, coolly clad in a lilac dress in a light floaty fabric, she was walking past the car parks at the entrance to the historic site when a long silver limousine pulled up beside her. His broad face expressionless, Damianos climbed out and flipped open the rear passenger door for her. 'Kyria Cozakis…'

Having stilled in astonishment at first glimpse of Nik's bodyguard, Olympia was frozen to the pavement. How on earth had she been found at such speed?

'Olympia…' A dark, deep familiar drawl murmured from the interior. 'I'll give you a count of five to join me inside the limo *without* argument.'

A furious flush lit Olympia's cheeks. Outraged at being addressed as if she were a spoilt child likely to throw a tantrum, she took a hasty couple of steps closer. 'Someone followed me off the yacht…right?'

'One,' Nik sounded, infuriating her even more.

'Someone's been spying on me. Well, I think that was really low and contemptible—'

'Two.'

Out of the corner of her eye, she noticed Damianos retreat back round the limo and fold into the front seat. 'Furthermore, I have plans of my own—'

'Three.'

'I just want to see the Alhambra…OK?'

'Four.'

'There's no way you are going to tell me to get in that car

when I don't want to, Nik Cozakis!' Olympia slung fierily, with her hands planted on her hips.

'Five…'

Snatching in a ragged breath, Olympia crossed her arms and thrust up her chin. Nik emerged in one fluid but forceful movement. Sheathed in a tailored suit the colour of pale honey, he looked spectacular, and, even mad as she was with him, her heartbeat quickened and her mouth ran dry. Taking note of the curious tourists nearby, Nik assumed a studious air of solicitude.

Lifting her into his arms with exaggerated care, he drawled with fake anxiety, 'You never could take the heat, darling…you need to lie down for a while. Preferably *under* me,' he completed for her ears alone.

Stowed inside the limo because she honestly didn't have the nerve to fight him in a public place, but incensed at the growling arrogance of that conclusion, Olympia gasped, 'I'm getting straight back out again—'

Slamming the door, Nik swung back to her, brilliant eyes hard and angry. 'You took your life in your hands when you left the security of the yacht yesterday!'

Olympia bridled. 'What on earth are you talking about?'

His lean, strong face set in grim lines, Nik continued to study her with unconcealed censure. 'Whether you like it or not, you are the wife of a very rich man and the granddaughter of another, and that makes you an extremely vulnerable target.'

'For what?'

'For kidnappers, thieves and aggressive paparazzi!' Nik spelt out with wrathful bite. 'The instant I learnt you had left *Aurora* alone, I was seriously worried about your personal safety! The crew member who followed you for your own protection was unable to report your whereabouts until late last night.'

Involuntarily, Olympia had paled. 'No thief would find anything worth stealing on me.'

'And how would you like to find yourself at the mercy of a gang of thieves who couldn't even get a Rolex watch for their trouble?' Nik demanded rawly.

Olympia's tummy curdled and she dropped her head. His genuine concern made her feel ashamed, for if she was truthful her primary objective in getting off the yacht had been to infuriate Nik with a taste of the same treatment he had given her. 'I wouldn't…I'm sorry, I honestly didn't think.'

Nik expelled a slow, fracturing hiss. 'At least you are all right…apart from your hair.'

'My hair?' The sudden change of subject disconcerted her.

Nik skimmed lean brown fingers down the foreshortened length of the glossy mahogany strands now hanging just below her shoulderblades. 'You butchered your beautiful hair. How could you *do* that?'

Hot pink flooded Olympia's cheeks. She hadn't been prepared for Nik to be that blunt, nor for the strength of his unconcealed regret.

'You knew how much I loved your hair.' Nik withdrew his hand with a heavy sigh. 'I suppose I'm lucky I didn't hold your throat in the same regard. No doubt you would have cut it and bled to death.'

It was ridiculous, but, feeling like a woman who had sacrificed her sole attraction, she found her eyes smarting with tears. 'It'll grow…' she heard herself say in a wobbly voice, even though she preferred her hair shorter and found it far easier to handle.

'So now we go and see the Alhambra,' Nik murmured flatly.

'No, never mind…you're not even dressed for—'

'I insist, *pethi mou*. Today we take up where we left off a week ago and start learning to be married.'

Olympia flicked a startled glance at him.

Dark, deepset eyes met hers levelly. 'I had some stuff to work out but I should not have stayed away for so long.'

With Damianos and another bodyguard trailing them at a

discreet distance, Nik and Olympia went off to explore the
Alhambra. It was a gorgeous day. The sun shone down on
wooded walks with the green freshness of spring. Olympia
was enchanted by all that she saw: the haunting inner courts
with their tranquil fountains and the sand-coloured towers
mirrored on the surface of still, silent pools.

They wandered through the lush gardens of the Generalife.
In a cool rose-shaded arbour, sunlight sparkling through the
drops of a water spout, Olympia glanced up and found Nik's
intent gaze welded to her.

'What?' she muttered self-consciously.

'You are quite unaware of your own power,' Nik asserted
with an amused shake of his dark head. 'In many ways, still
so innocent. That day in my office I would have recognised
that if I hadn't been so angry with you.'

Olympia tautened. She recognised the change in his outlook with slow, wondering relief. In his time away from her,
Nik seemed to have shaken free of his anger and his bitterness and his desire to wound. 'I did *try* to tell you that nothing happ—'

'No...' Nik pressed a cool forefinger against her eagerly
parted lips. 'Leave it all in the past, where it belongs.'

Her eyes shadowed. 'But—'

'No more bad memories.' Brushing back the smooth hair
falling across her cheekbone as she frowned, he murmured
grimly, 'We were just kids, and kids do stupid things when
they get in too deep too young.'

For a split second she wanted to protest that she hadn't
done anything stupid, had indeed done nothing to deserve the
condemnation she had suffered, but she sensed that it was
neither the time nor the place to press that argument again.
Nik had moved on, and in the short term so must she, unless
she was prepared to risk the promise of a new and better
understanding. As she lifted her head again, she collided with
smouldering dark golden eyes.

Instantly she was divorced from everything but her intense

awareness of him. His lean, lithe powerful physique, the proud tilt of his well-groomed dark head, the strong cheekbones which stamped his bronzed features with such strength and character and the wicked sensuality of his beautiful mouth.

'I want you, *yineka mou*,' Nik admitted with a boldness that shook her, his brilliant gaze roaming over her shapely figure with explicit hunger.

Just as suddenly, the atmosphere crackled with electric energy.

Olympia felt her face burn and her skin dampen. All sound around them was distanced, just as if the world had stopped. No longer did she hear the soft rush of playing water, the distant hum of voices in the hot still air. Her heartbeat thudded as she snatched in a stark breath. Embarrassment seized her as she became conscious of the heaviness of her breasts and the tormenting throb of her swollen nipples.

His hands on her tense shoulders, Nik drew her closer, a world of intimate knowledge in his stunning eyes. She trembled, the power of every sense heightened, an almost choking excitement currenting through her. But she found it unbearable to be held and not touched.

'It may hurt to wait, but anticipation makes the pleasure all the keener,' Nik muttered thickly, linking his fingers tautly to hers and urging her back into the sunlight.

Later she didn't recall that walk back to the limo, only that it left her with legs that felt as weak as cottonwool. Damianos mentioned something about lunch and Nik vented a ragged laugh. She looked at her watch, but she couldn't interest herself enough to focus and think. Nothing mattered but the burn of Nik's jaguar eyes on her, the possessive hold of his hand, a proximity which was as much a torture to her as a necessity.

She leant towards him in the back of the limo. His fabulous bone structure taut below his golden skin, he held her back. 'Not enough time,' he spelt out with roughened urgency. 'I don't want to be interrupted.'

Olympia snatched in a wavering breath as the limousine sped away. The silence sizzled. She was trembling. She skimmed a fascinated glance down at their still linked hands and felt as if her heart was expanding inside her constricted chest. A wealth of emotion was welling up within her. Fierce longing mingled with even fiercer hope.

For the first time in a month she truly understood herself. She didn't question from where her feelings had come, or even how, she simply accepted the reality of their existence. She *loved* Nik Cozakis. Not with the uncritical adulation of her youth but with the deep desperation of a woman, who knew the pitfalls and the probable hurt that lay ahead. Love wasn't on the agenda in their marriage deal.

The limousine pulled up in front of a palatial building built of ancient weathered stone. Nik tugged her out into the sunlight. With an inclination of his imperious dark head he acknowledged the respectful greeting of an older man standing on the steps and swept her straight through the imposing entrance into a dim interior. On his impatient passage to the stairs she glimpsed ornate dark antique furniture and a vast Persian rug lying on worn flagstones. From the stairs, she saw upturned curious faces studying them across the vast reception hall, and finally realised that they were in a very grand and no doubt very exclusive hotel.

She coloured. 'People are staring at us—'

The shift of one broad shoulder signifying his supreme uninterest in the curiosity of strangers, Nik strode across the magnificent landing. A maid waiting there bobbed the equivalent of a curtsy and hastened to throw wide the double doors of a beautifully furnished reception room.

'This is really lovely—' Olympia began, just a tiny bit taken aback by the indecent speed with which they had arrived within reach of a bedroom and striving to play it cool.

But Nik swung her back to him, cupped her cheekbones with hard, impatient hands and drove his lips down on hers with an explosive hunger that blew her away. She clung to his suit jacket to stay upright, whimpering low in her throat in startled response as his tongue stabbed sensually deep into the tender interior of her mouth.

'Theos mou...I need to be inside you,' Nik groaned in frustration as she lay against him, struggling to get air back into her lungs, her whole body weak with aftershocks and the kind of anticipation that reduced all self-discipline to rubble.

He gathered her up into his arms and strode with purpose into the bedroom. Lowering her back on to her feet, he pulled down the zip on her dress and brushed it from her shoulders so that it slid into a heap round her ankles. He scanned her scantily clad figure with heavily lidded golden eyes that made her entire skin surface burn and tingle and slowly settled her back on to the foot of the big bed.

Struggling to concentrate, Olympia muttered anxiously, 'Shouldn't we have checked in at Reception?'

Nik frowned. 'Why?'

'Because that's what people usually do...*isn't it*?'

''Not when they own the hotel.'

'Oh...' Olympia watched him discard his superb tailored suit with the same sort of pent-up excitement she might have felt at the highest point of a rollercoaster ride. Her heart was hammering so hard it was literally a challenge to breathe. Her tongue couldn't form words. Her body trembled, awake and eager and utterly outside her control.

Across the room, she encountered dark golden eyes that made her head spin. She was weak with a wanting so powerful it hurt, but still she attempted to be sensible. 'We...we should talk first,' she whispered unevenly.

'At this particular moment?' Nik demanded in frank disbelief. 'No chance!'

Hot-faced, she surveyed him, her heartbeat pounding at an insane rate in her own eardrums, her swollen lips parted, her mouth dry as a bone.

'This past week has felt like six months,' Nik imparted,

his Greek accent thick as molasses as he stripped off his boxer shorts and strode back to her, naked and glorious.

'I feel like I'm going to die of excitement,' Olympia mumbled in honest shame, shattered by the strength of the craving he could rouse in her. With his eyes, with his words, with the hard, sleek urgent masculinity of his magnificent physique. He was pure, packaged sexual enticement at that moment, and she was enthralled.

As he came down to her, Nik treated her to a primal smile of promise. 'Not yet, *pethi mou...*but soon.'

Already she ached for him, feverishly aware of the hot pulse between her thighs. She held herself very still as he skimmed the straps of her bra out of his path and eased away the embroidered cups to expose her full breasts and their prominent pink peaks.

Venting a groan of satisfaction, Nik captured a sensitive bud between his lips and laved it with the tip of his tongue. With a gasp of reaction, she arched her hips off the bed. Raising his head, Nik pushed his hands beneath her hips and removed her briefs. He let his tongue delve into the sucked-in hollow of her navel while his skilled fingers went on to explore the straining length of one taut thigh. She jerked, almost out of her mind with excitement. Then without warning found herself wondering if it was always like this for him with a woman, indeed, if he was the same with other women, and she tensed, coldness touching the fire burning through her.

She looked up at him, lifted an unsteady hand to stroke her fingers through the black hair she had already tousled and let her fingertips trail back down over one high, proud cheekbone to the firm curve of his chiselled mouth.

For a split second, eyes as dark as jet assailed hers. Nik ravished her mouth with his again. It drove her mind blank, shut out everything but the all-consuming power of sensation and her own needy response. Casting aside her bra, he directed his attention back to the tender flesh he had already sensitised. She squirmed and gasped out loud, the heat building in the pit of her stomach sending a message of fire to the very heart of her.

'*Theos*...if I had touched you in the car, I would have had you,' Nik swore with a ragged laugh. 'Sometimes you turn me on so fast and hard, I feel like an animal.'

'I want you too...' she confided unsteadily, desperate need digging talon claws of impatience into her.

He touched her then, where she so needed to be touched. He discovered the swollen damp welcome that already awaited him and with a hungry growl he shifted and pushed her thighs back with determined hands.

She saw the wildness in him as he came down over her. It was a savage hunger for possession that melted her skin to her bones. His cheekbones were taut and flushed, his brilliant eyes blazing. She lay there pliant and exposed, exulting in his forceful maleness with every fibre of her being.

'I am burning for this,' Nik intoned quietly, with feeling fervour.

He entered her with a single driving thrust that wrenched a keening moan of shaken response from her. Buried deep inside her, he gazed down at her with burning satisfaction and rasped, 'You feel like hot silk. *This*...being with you again...is all I've thought about since I left you.'

She couldn't speak. The intimacy of his bold possession brought a wave of delight that was blindingly intense. Every inch of her quivering body was leaping with crazy excitement, and with his every virile stroke the level of her craving for him increased. Heart banging, pulses pounding, she clung to him. Wild sensation overwhelmed her with hot, drowning pleasure. Then a shooting starburst of explosive heat consumed the last of her awareness and left her freefalling from mindless ecstasy back to the real world again.

Hauling back the covers on the bed in the aftermath, Nik swept her up and laid her down on an exquisitely cool sheet. As he urged her back into his arms, Nik vented a husky laugh. 'It was worth thinking about all week as well, *yineka mou*,' he confided, with very male appreciation.

Olympia's heartbeat was only slowly subsiding to a less maddened pace. She discovered that once more she could think. Her joy at being with Nik again spilt over into momentary sadness, for, looking back ten years, she realised that she now saw a different picture. At seventeen, her ultimate dream guy had asked her out and put an engagement ring on her finger. Nik had genuinely been attracted to her, Nik had genuinely loved her, but she hadn't been equal to the starring role in what had felt too much like a fairy story. So, aided and abetted by her grandfather and Katerina, she had questioned the dream, doubted the dream, and ended up losing the dream through her own sense of unworthiness.

Nik shifted with sinuous sensuality against her. The faraway look of regret in Olympia's eyes was replaced by one of shaken sexual awareness. In the wake of that acknowledgement of loss, she was gripped by a fierce desire to make the most of every moment and live it to the full. 'I loved you so much—'

'Did you?' His lush lashes dipped, screening his spectacular eyes to the merest glimmer of reflective light.

She sensed Nik's withdrawal and knew that once again she had got too close to the fire. She wanted to offer him feverish confirmation and tell him that she loved him still, but fear and pride held her back from that brink. Unable to voice what was on her mind, she took refuge in touching him instead. She wrapped her arms round him in an almost clumsy gesture of affection.

'You're driving me insane with all this intense rave-from-the-grave stuff...it's like the clock stopped ticking for you when you were seventeen,' Nik framed with blunt censure, sliding over on to his back and carrying her with him, rearranging her with confident hands to his own satisfaction.

Olympia was desperately hurt by an accusation that was, she registered belatedly, all too accurate. Yet on their wedding night *she* had been the one to accuse Nik of being obsessed with the past. Now their roles had been reversed. But, perhaps mercifully, her weak body was already reacting with brazen hussy efficiency to the urgent arousal of his. A wave of responsive heat gripped her, blurring all thought. Her breasts were crushed into his chest, her tender nipples tingling at that sensation. She was so close to him, but not anything like close enough.

Nik surveyed her with deceptively indolent sexuality and teasing expectation. 'Now I would like to demonstrate all the many wonderful ways I can give you incredible pleasure, Kyria Cozakis.'

His supreme confidence blazed over her like a scorching golden aura, and she could not hold back the tender smile curving her mouth.

CHAPTER EIGHT

FOUR weeks later, Olympia sat up, sipping the iced water she had poured from the flask by the bed.

They had arrived at Nik's magnificent villa on the island of Kritos late the night before. Olympia had slept well, but now she felt slightly dizzy and nauseous. And she knew *why*, didn't she? Frowning at that acknowledgement, Olympia tugged on a light robe and slid back the doors that gave access to the superb balcony beyond the bedroom. A sea breeze wafted in, the cooling air bliss on her clammy skin. As the voile drapes she had brushed back fluttered, she stilled them with a careful hand and glanced back at the bed.

Nik was still asleep in an indolent sprawl of long, lithe bronzed limbs, the pale linen sheet tangled round his lean hips. A dreamy smile curved her mouth. After an entire month spend cruising the Mediterranean, she was happier than she had ever dreamt of being again. Yet if that was true, why was she holding back on telling Nik that she was pregnant?

It was only eight, but Olympia was too restive to return to bed and went for a bath. Lying back in the scented water, she recalled the terms of their marriage deal and sighed heavily. Nik had been breaking those same rules for the past month. He was *living* with her! Although he had flown in several staff, and begun making use of his office on board *Aurora*, he still spent an enormous amount of time with her. Now that they were back on dry land again, she saw no reason why that shouldn't continue.

Towelling herself dry, she acknowledged that recently Nik had indulged her every wish to the hilt. Such freedom of choice had rather gone to her head, for all her life she had longed to travel and see the sights she had only read about. Over the past weeks the yacht had docked at Majorca, Corsica, Sardinia and finally Sicily. In retrospect, a bewildering jumble of memories engulfed Olympia. Sunlit beaches, shimmering seas, twisting roads and extravagant and beautiful scenery.

Certain memories stood out in sharp definition. Nik linking his hand with hers as they walked through the exclusive resort of Porto Cervo in Sardinia a week ago…his fury at the sudden appearance of paparazzi with flashing cameras and the protective way he had screened her from that unpleasant invasion. Nik laughing, teasing, caring and attentive in all sorts of little ways. Nik telling her off for not wearing a higher factor suncream when she got burned, his concern palpable. And, oh, at least a hundred memories of his lovemaking. Occasionally gentle, sometimes wild, but always passionate.

He loved her body. She accepted that now. At every opportunity he made her feel sexually irresistible. There had been days when her plans to explore new places hadn't even got off the ground, days when Nik had taken one incredulous glance at the itinerary she had mapped out and rebelled, taking her back to bed instead. Nights when they'd never made the dinner table and had eaten in the early hours.

Yet still she was in no hurry to share the news that she had conceived their first child. It was forty-eight hours since Nik had insisted that a doctor examine her sunburned shoulders. Conscious that she hadn't had a period since before their wedding, Olympia had made full use of that consultation. A brief examination and one little test had followed, and then the confirmation had been given: she was going to have a baby. She was both thrilled and terrified. Before their marriage Nik had made her getting pregnant sound like a likely halfway post to divorce.

And what if they didn't really *have* a new understanding? How could she tell for sure? Nik never mentioned the future.

Nik never mentioned the deal he had forced upon her. They could well have been living in a time capsule, where only the immediate present existed. And for now he was charming, the ultimate in entertaining company. But then why shouldn't he be? she thought with a sinking heart. He had already got her pregnant in record time.

'I've got a complaint to make. Where *were* you when I woke up?'

Olympia jumped halfway out of her skin and spun round from the mirror. Nik was poised in the doorway, black hair wildly tousled, strong jawline dark with stubble, slumbrous dark golden eyes gleaming, a wolfish grin of amusement curving his mouth. He looked heartbreakingly gorgeous.

'Nik—'

'I've ordered breakfast...for later.' Strolling across the spectacular mosaic-tiled bathroom, Nik closed his hands over hers and urged her into his arms. 'Join me in the shower and tell me who you were daydreaming about...it had better have been me, *pethi mou.*'

Delicate colour burnished her cheeks. She buried her face in his shoulder, loving the hot, musky evocative scent of his brown skin. 'Who else?'

Disposing of her robe, he swept her under the shower with him. 'I have so much work to catch up on,' he muttered raggedly between hard, drugging kisses that left her taut and trembling, caught up and inflamed by his hungry urgency. 'We have guests coming too. *Theos mou*...to hell with all that!'

A long while later, they breakfasted out on the beautiful stone terrace, shaded by tulip trees and a lush, colourful tangle of bougainvillea. The day was glorious, hot and still, the very light golden. In every direction the views were breathtaking. Set high on a mountainside studded with cypress groves, which stretched down to the blue green waters of the Aegean, the villa was surrounded by lush natural gardens which blended into the landscape.

In the distance she could see the harbour, adorned by a picturesque collection of houses, and the most lovely little church with a domed campanile. In the deep natural bay *Aurora* towered like a giant ocean-going liner in a sea of brightly coloured fishing boats. From her first glimpse of Kritos by moonlight the night before, Olympia had been utterly enchanted.

Only then recalling Nik's reference to guests, Olympia frowned in sudden mingled dismay and amusement at her own inability to concentrate earlier. 'You mentioned guests... who's coming and when?'

'Markos Stapoulos and his wife, Samantha. She's British. I think you'll like her,' Nik drawled levelly. 'They couldn't make our wedding because Markos's father was ill, but they're flying in to lunch with us. They should be here in about half an hour.'

Olympia had already stiffened. Ten years back, Markos Stapoulos had been Nik's best friend. Filled with strong discomfiture at the prospect of meeting him again, she said sharply, 'I suppose Markos knows all about that pathetic car park story as well!'

If ever a silence could have been said to sizzle like the string leading to a stick of dynamite, the endless yawning silence which followed that exclamation sizzled.

Studying her with stunned and disconcerted eyes, Nik rammed his hands down on the surface of the table and leapt up to his full intimidating height. '*Christos!* Do you think I dined out on that particular story?' he grated, with an explosive fury that shook her. 'Apart from your grandfather, only my parents and Katerina know about that night!'

As Olympia watched, pale but unbowed, Nik strode out from beneath the shade of the tulip trees and into full sunlight. He swung back to face her, his bone structure rigid beneath his bronzed skin, brilliant dark eyes hard with condemnation as he spread his arms in a striking show of raw incomprehension. 'Why are you dragging all this up again?'

'Because you still won't either listen to or believe in my version,' Olympia whispered ruefully. 'And I resent that.'

A dark line of colour scored Nik's hard cheekbones. '*Theos mou*...you have no right to resent anything! You're damn lucky I decided to put that tawdry episode behind us and appreciate you for the woman you are today!'

'If you put it behind you, why are you still shouting at me?'

'I...am...not...shouting,' Nik asserted, with such thickened and challenged self-restraint behind that assurance that she could barely distinguish his words.

'Good, because I was never with Lukas and I'm going to keep on telling you that until you listen!'

'But I'll *never* believe you.' His black eyes glittered like banked twin fires over her, his derision unconcealed. 'I remember the way you looked at me the morning after. You were guilty and proud of it!'

And Olympia remembered her bitter, silent defiance and recognised that Nik's bone-deep conviction that she was now lying stemmed as much from what he had seen in her as from the nonsense he had been told. A great weariness enfolded her then.

'Yet looking back, knowing what I know now...it was nothing!' Nik shrugged with expressive dismissal. 'I should have said it before now, but naturally being your first lover made up—'

'It made up for so much you vanished for a whole week!' Olympia slotted in. *You have no right to resent anything.*

She shivered, trembling fingers curling round her glass of fresh orange juice. Nice to finally find out what lay behind the smooth and charming façade. A stubborn Greek male as unforgiving as a rock that stood through the centuries, weathered but immovable. She was so furious with him she had to weld her back to the seat to stop herself from flying upright and screaming back at him.

'Why don't you just tell me exactly what you *did* do with Lukas?' Nik demanded with sudden splintering force.

In total shock at that blunt invitation, Olympia's eyes opened very wide.

In response, Nik jerked both his hands up in the air in a speaking gesture of savage frustration. 'It's *your* fault I'm thinking like this again!' he condemned with raw violence. 'Why the hell couldn't you just leave it alone?'

He strode past the table and then stilled, wide shoulders rigid beneath the fine, expensive cloth of his well-cut jacket. He swung back, dug something from his pocket. He tossed a leather jeweller's box down on the table in front of her. It was a careless, understated move that nonetheless contrived to shout censure, reproach and arrogant male superiority. 'I was planning to give you that after breakfast.'

Olympia had never liked one-upmanship. 'What's in the box...a *truth* drug?'

Nik swore long and low in guttural Greek and strode back into the villa.

Olympia flipped open the box and found herself looking at an exquisite diamond-studded locket. She lifted it out, more or less to occupy her shaking hands, and flipped it open. Inside were two tiny photos of her mother and her grandfather. She was incredibly touched by that thoughtful and personalised extra. Had she overreacted or had he? Who was more guilty? The tears overflowed.

Resolving to pull herself together, Olympia went back indoors. Passing through the superb galleried hall, she went upstairs to their bedroom. What did Nik feel for her? Did he feel *anything* of any importance? Or was she just another bed partner for a highly-sexed male? Was the dark side of Nik's volatile temperament getting a kick out of the fact that she couldn't resist him? For, if he cared at all, how could he still distrust her to such an extent? That hurt her very much. It also seemed to make a complete charade of the wonderful weeks they had spent together.

In search of her make-up, Olympia reached for the handbag she had used the night before. It was a capacious holdall, and with a moan of impatience she tipped out the entire contents on to the bed. In the act of reaching for her cosmetics purse, she stilled in surprise to study the medium-sized brown envelope which had also fallen out of her bag. The envelope was sealed and she had never seen it before.

With a frown, she tore it open. A newspaper cutting and a pair of glossy colour snaps tumbled out on to the smooth silk bedspread. Olympia stared fixedly at the topmost photo, its rather fuzzy quality suggesting the use of a long-range camera. It was Gisele Bonner, lying topless on a sun lounger in the arms of a male who looked remarkably like Nik. Remarkably. She peered at that male image with straining eyes and then bent to examine the other photograph. Another shot of a bare bosom she would sooner not have seen, she conceded, with what felt like a hysterical laugh building like a giant bubble in her tight throat. But in the foreground of that second photo, now standing full face to that clever, intrusive camera lens, she saw Nik. Not a male who bore a remarkable resemblance to Nik but a male who was without a single shadow of doubt Nik Cozakis!

Her heart sounded a dulled, thunderous thud. Without warning, the door at the other side of the room opened. 'Olympia...?' It was Nik's rich dark drawl.

Without the slightest thought or hesitation, Olympia flung herself face down on the bed across the photos, the newspaper cutting, her handbag and its jumbled contents.

Nik drew to a halt and regarded her prone position with a slight frown. 'Are you feeling OK?'

'Fine...'

When she made no move to get up, Nik hunkered down by the side of the bed, his stunning dark eyes level. 'You've been crying—'

'No, I haven't been.'

'Liar,' he groaned, one forefinger gently tracing a silvered tear-track marking her cheek. 'I'm sorry I lost my head. I just can't think straight when you mention…' His lean strong face shadowed and darkened, his tension returning. 'I know it's not reasonable, but just please don't mention it again. It makes me…unreasonable,' he selected, after a long hesitation and perceptible difficulty in coming up with an alternative word.

'Yes…' She wasn't really listening; the facts of that stupid business with Lukas ten years back now seemed unimportant. She was staring deep into Nik's gorgeous dark golden eyes and praying, praying that the photos she was concealing from him were *old* photos, sent by his vindictive ex-mistress merely to taunt and distress his new wife.

'Are you sure you're OK?'

Olympia's fingernails curled into the bedspread. 'Just give me five minutes to fix my face—'

'Did you like the locket? Damianos said lockets went out with parasols and fans, but I thought it was *you*…'

'It's me,' she confirmed tightly.

His brows pleating, Nik vaulted slowly back upright.

As soon as he had gone, Olympia rose into a crouch to snatch at the crumpled newspaper cutting lying beneath her. Sinking back on to her knees, she spread it, surprised to see that there were two photos set side by side in the cutting. One the pool scene featuring Nik and Gisele in a clinch and the other of Nik and Olympia emerging from the church after their wedding.

As Olympia registered the proof that the picture of Nik about to snog Gisele must have been taken after she herself had married him, she sucked in oxygen in a great gulp, perspiration dampening her brow. Her stomach curdled. Sick, deep shock engulfed her. Beneath the pool photo, in confirmation of her worst suspicions, ran the immortal words; *'Nik Cozakis breaks his honeymoon in the Med to comfort his mistress.'*

That first week they had been married, the week when he

had left her alone on the yacht. When else? Nik had been with his mistress, Gisele Bonner. A mistress not former but *current*. Getting up from the bed, Olympia thrust the photos and the cutting back into her handbag. Then she hovered like a sleepwalker. She went into the bathroom to freshen up. But when she got there she discovered she hadn't brought her cosmetics purse with her and she had to walk back to the bed to fetch it. Then she found that her hands were shaking so badly she was powdering her eyes instead of her shiny nose.

Who had planted that envelope in her bag? Her maid? Five weeks earlier, greeted on the yacht on her wedding day with that 'Compete if you can!' message and the magazine article on Gisele, Olympia had believed the young Greek woman was innocent of any involvement. Now she was less naive. Only her maid had enjoyed such free access to her state room. Only her maid could have easily put anything inside her handbag. But right then the identity of Gisele's helpmate seemed relatively unimportant. It *had* to be Gisele who was doing this to her, didn't it? Surely Katerina could not be responsible for these photos as well?

Olympia was so shattered she could barely think straight. I'm pregnant. I'm pregnant by him now, she kept on thinking dizzily, panic threatening. When she heard the whirring, clacking beat of a helicopter getting louder overhead, she had to force herself to leave the bedroom; their guests were arriving. As she went downstairs, she pressed a tremulous hand to her pounding brow. She breathed in very slowly and deeply. She had to get a hold of herself fast, because there was no way, absolutely no way, that she could confront Nik with other people around.

Elegant in her peacock-blue shift dress, Olympia stared across the stone terrace at Nik as he approached the helipad to welcome the arrivals. In a lightweight suit the colour of honey, superbly tailored to outline his broad shoulders and long, long legs, Nik looked sensational. Her heart lurched. A male possessed of devastating attraction who might well have no more sensibility than an animal in the mating season when it came to satisfying his own sexual inclinations. Undersexed he wasn't. She knew that for herself. Her husband, her lover. Time she came back to the real world again, she decided numbly...

Nik Cozakis was a Greek tycoon. One of a rarefied breed of very rich and powerful men, little given to the virtues of self-denial and fidelity. On the very day Nik had blackmailed her into agreeing to *his* marital terms he had said with cool satisfaction, 'I also get a wife who really knows how to behave herself, a wife who never, ever questions where I go or what I do because we have a business deal, *not* a marriage.' Just when had she chosen to forget those horribly revealing words of warning? At what point had she chosen to ditch all memory of that ruthless blackmail and those threats?

Her tummy tied itself into knots and her fingers closed in tightly on themselves. Only as Markos Stapoulos and his wife emerged from their helicopter did Olympia move forward to stand by Nik's side. Markos was a short, thickset cheerful bear of a man, already going grey, Samantha an effervescent Scottish redhead.

Olympia was grateful for the other couple's enlivening presence. She needed time, time in which to get a grip on her flailing emotions. On several occasions she became conscious of Nik's dark, questioning gaze on her and she cursed his perceptive powers. She couldn't bring herself to look at him, and no doubt he had noticed the brittle quality she could hear in her own voice as she endeavoured to respond appropriately to Samantha's friendly chatter.

After lunch, the two men vanished into Nik's office.

'Business, everything is always *business* with Greek men!' Samantha shook her head in rueful acceptance.

'How did you meet Markos?' Olympia asked, just a little of her highwire tension evaporating with Nik's removal from the scene.

'I was a nurse in the London clinic where he had his appendix out. Between you and me and the gatepost, he was terrified! That was three years ago.' Smiling, Samantha relaxed back into her well-upholstered seat. 'You have no idea how much more comfortable I feel here now that Nik has a wife too.'

'You must've met Gisele Bonner,' Olympia heard herself say, and it was as much of a shock to her to hear that comment escape as it was to her companion, who stilled in surprise. 'Please...just forget I said that. I really wasn't fishing!' Olympia hastened to assert.

'No, you can say anything to me. I *do* understand how you must feel.' With an air of ready sympathy which increased Olympia's embarrassment, Samantha leant forward and began to talk in a confidential manner. 'Ex-girlfriends who look as stunning as Gisele and who continue to hog the headlines long after their sell-by date are hard to swallow. Of course you don't like that. The first time we met Gisele, Markos was *mesmerised*...I could have strangled him! I didn't speak to him for a week!'

Olympia felt torn into two, both wanting and not wanting to hear more.

'Gisele's clever, and very ambitious. She got her claws into Nik and hung on in there even when his attention strayed!' her companion divulged.

Olympia nodded, wondering in dulled horror whether she was supposed to be cheered by the news that Nik hadn't been faithful to his mistress either.

'Gisele knows how to please a man. That was the secret of her staying power.' Samantha pulled a face. 'Have you ever met a Greek male who *didn't* love having his ego stroked by a woman who hangs on his every word and treats him like a god?'

Olympia shook her head and closely studied her tightly linked hands.

'You really shouldn't be worrying about her, Olympia.'

'I'm not.' Olympia was beyond worrying. Having learnt the secret of Gisele's success, she knew her marriage was over. The chances of her treating Nik like a god in the near future were slim to none.

'Nik lives very much in the limelight and Gisele adored sharing it with him. It did a lot for her career. I bet she was behind that ridiculous story printed in that downmarket tabloid last month,' the other woman continued with visible distaste. 'But who on earth would believe that Nik was with *her* when you and Nik had only just gone off on your honeymoon?'

'Who?' Olympia echoed with a sickly smile. Yet that was exactly what Nik had done. After one night, he had abandoned his bride in favour of his mistress. A tiny tremor ran through her tense frame.

'That kind of horrible lie appearing in newsprint makes me grateful that Markos and I aren't glitzy enough to be a target for the paparazzi.' Samantha sighed.

At that point Nik strode in through the doors standing wide on the stone terrace. Olympia jerked in dismay and liquid spilled from the glass in her hand, staining her dress. 'Oh, heck...' she mumbled, rising hurriedly from her seat with averted eyes. 'Excuse me, I'll have to change.'

'We've all been invited to join a wedding party in the village,' Nik imparted.

'I'd love that,' Samantha responded warmly. 'But did Markos mention that we have to leave by seven?'

Slipping quietly from the room, Olympia breathed in deep. A *wedding*? For a dangerous split-second, the crushing pressure of the emotional turmoil she was struggling to contain threatened to break its boundaries. Like a living nightmare, she saw warning flashes of what might happen if she lost control. She would shout, she would scream, she would break things. In response to the rising level of her distress, she felt violent. Angry, bitter, outraged. Why couldn't he love her? Why couldn't he love her the way she loved him? Would this day, this enforced pretence of harmony for the benefit of their guests *never* end? she wondered wretchedly.

Upstairs, she wrenched an elaborate backless black cocktail dress with a bolero jacket from a hanger, knowing that she would be expected to dress up for such an occasion. Having been welcomed ashore by a party of villagers when they arrived the night before, Olympia was under no illusions as to Nik's status on the island of Kritos. If Gisele treated Nik Cozakis like a god, the islanders treated him like their king!

He had made island life viable for another generation. He had rebuilt the school, brought in an extra teacher, dredged the silted-up harbour and persuaded a doctor to take up residence in the state-of-the-art surgery he had supplied as a lure. He had also allowed the development of a small exclusive resort on the other side of the island, which was providing employment for many of the younger people. He had done more for Kritos in five years than his father had done in his entire lifetime. And, in true heroic tradition, Olympia thought bitterly, Nik had personally told her none of those things. Markos Stapoulos had let those facts drop over lunch. But then Markos had always *hugely* admired Nik.

'Olympia...'

Olympia froze and slowly turned. Nik leant back against the bedroom door to close it. His lean, strong face taut, black eyes chillingly intent, he surveyed her. 'What the hell is the matter with you?'

'I beg your pardon?'

'Don't be facetious!' Nik countered with biting derision. 'You can't treat me like the invisible man without making our guests uncomfortable. Hospitality is a serious matter to all Greeks, a service we undertake with pride and pleasure. I can only be ashamed of a wife behaving like a sulky little brat!'

Olympia shivered and clenched her teeth together.

'And don't you *dare* give me that little fishwife look!' Nik growled, incensed.

Burning colour mantling her cheeks, her hands coiled into tight, hurting fists, Olympia murmured thickly, 'Maybe you should have asked Gisele Bonner to be your hostess instead.'

'You have a point. Gisele never let me down in front of my friends,' Nik responded, without a second of hesitation.

'That was really low, Nik...' Olympia whispered unsteadily, shaken even in the mood she was in by that smooth retaliation.

His stubborn jawline hardened. 'No woman treats me as you have today. We had a stupid argument and I apologised sincerely for my part in it. I have no time and even less patience for the way you're behaving now!'

Stiff-backed, Olympia spun away to lift the bolero lying on the bed. 'Go to hell...' she said succinctly.

A hand like an iron vice closed over her taut shoulder and turned her back. Nik gazed down at her with eyes as hot as golden flames. '*Christos*...do you have a death wish?' he grated incredulously. 'Or is it just that you don't like your own sex? Am I getting the big freeze because Samantha was bantering with me over lunch?'

Olympia was trembling. Nik was emanating rage in sizzling waves. 'I don't know what you're talking about—'

'You couldn't make even a polite pretence of forgiving Katerina either! Was that because she once had a crush on me?' Nik demanded. 'I want to know what the problem is. Is it jealousy that makes you act like this?'

Olympia dredged her eyes from his and focused on his caramel silk tie. 'You'd better go downstairs and join our guests again—'

'Markos knows I'm mad with you. *Theos mou*...I will go nowhere until you tell me what is the matter with you!' Nik swore in a savage undertone, sliding long fingers into the glossy fall of her hair and tipping up her face to his when she would have looked away. 'This morning you were smiling, laughing...*happy*!'

The tension in the atmosphere pulsed like a ticking time bomb. Against her will, she met scorching dark golden eyes and her heartbeat accelerated, her breathing quickening. She read the blunt masculine bewilderment in his angry gaze and something twisted inside her, filling her with wild despair and pain. 'Let...go...of...me,' she framed jerkily.

'I don't think so, *yineka mou*,' Nik breathed, lowering his arrogant dark head and prying her lips apart with the driving force of his mouth.

It was the very last thing Olympia had expected. She wasn't prepared. She had no time to muster her defences. The fierce turmoil inside her ignited as if he had thrown a match into a bale of hay. Shock flashed through her, and then suddenly she found that her hands were biting into his shoulders and she was kissing him back in a devastating melding of fury and hatred and hunger.

Tipping her back on to the bed, Nik pinned her arms to the mattress and plundered the tender interior of her mouth with an erotic urgency that drove her halfway out of her mind. She couldn't think. Her pent-up feelings were finding vent in a primal passion that smashed all boundaries, leaving her at the mercy of what felt like an uncontrollable need.

'You are mine...' Nik rasped, jack-knifing back from her to thrust up the skirt of her dress and hook his fingers to the waistband of her panties. He wrenched her out of them with unashamed impatience.

And she lay there quivering, every nerve-ending crying out for the satisfaction only he could give. Nothing else mattered, nothing but the desperate craving which had tightened her nipples to distended points and set up an agonising throbbing ache between her thighs.

'You understand this OK...' Nik gritted, running his burning, intent gaze over her, his scorching hunger hot as fire licking at her super-sensitive skin.

He came back to her with a driving kiss that consumed her. He was rough, and she had never known him rough before, and he excited her beyond belief. She was out of control, but so was he and she loved that. It answered the wildness leaping through her. He was hard and hot and full, and he sank into her tender welcoming flesh with a forceful maleness that made her sob out his name in ecstasy. Her back arched as the blinding excitement peaked on a shivering storming tide of mindless pleasure.

In the aftermath, she opened her eyes and blinked.

For a split-second, as Nik stared down at her, she saw a shell-shocked look in his stunning dark deepset eyes that could only have mirrored her own. Rolling off her without a word, he headed for the bathroom. She lay there immobile, struggling to breathe again, feeling ravished, feeling the sweet, heavy satiation of her own body with shattered recognition. She tottered upright and smoothed down her dress with unsteady hands.

Tossing the towel he had dried his face with on the floor, Nik studied her from the bathroom doorway. 'Come here...' he urged raggedly, opening his arms with pure Greek expansiveness.

'You don't need to say sorry...I liked it,' Olympia admitted, half under her breath, her voice wobbling.

He crossed the room, curved an arm round her and bent his dark head to brush his mouth sensually across one feverishly flushed cheekbone. 'Sometimes you make me so angry I could self-destruct. I can handle that...but I can't handle what I don't understand,' he murmured in a raw-edged undertone, his accent very thick.

'It's OK...' And she meant it, but not in the way she knew he would read it. She loved him more than she had ever loved anything or anybody. But she also knew at that moment that she would never live with him again, never let him touch her again, that there had never been any big decision to make. Only her own weak and fearful reluctance to confront reality had allowed her to spend a few hours in a turmoil of indecision.

'It's not like I...like I don't care about you,' Nik said gruffly, after a long silence which had screeched with his tension, his struggle to find something he could bear to say. 'You're my wife.'

He hovered for a moment, as if he hoped that statement would dredge some response from her. When it didn't, he left the room.

Olympia studied her panties where they lay on the carpet. She wasn't shocked by that wild bout of sex they had just shared. She had wanted him, needed him, and had briefly found an outlet for an agony beyond what she could bear.

And Nik? Nik was terrific at handing out orders and reading the riot act, marvellous at sticking to the light and charming in conversation, but when serious communication beckoned Nik Cozakis was almost as inarticulate as a toddler. So grabbing her and kissing her like Neanderthal man and venting his emotions in a purely physical way had provided a necessary escape route. Odd, she reflected, that he should be so attuned to her that he had seen right through her efforts to behave normally. By rights, Nik should have been easily taken in.

But he didn't *hate* her anymore. A shaken laugh escaped Olympia as she restored her appearance to one of respectability. She thought of her baby, the baby that Nik had ensured she conceived. She pressed her hand protectively against her stomach. No wonder Nik had spent four whole weeks *living* with her! Had he marooned her in separate accommodation and only made flying visits to her bed, getting her pregnant might well have taken months. But all that was over now. The deed was done. She would love her baby, she would look after her baby, but she would not give house-room to a husband who had slept with another woman.

Before she went downstairs, she marvelled at the strange tranquillity of acceptance which now enfolded her. She found the housekeeper in the kitchen and gave her clear and concise instructions; Nik would hate her again by the end of the evening.

They drove down to the village taverna, where the wedding festivities were in full swing, in a Toyota Landcruiser with Nik at the wheel. Settled at a large table in the seat of honour, Nik found his attention much in demand, and Markos swiftly became involved too, in what was an overwhelmingly male-dominated dialogue.

Beside Olympia, Samantha released a little gurgle of laughter.

Olympia glanced at her.

Samantha's eyes danced with amusement. 'Do you know what I was just thinking? What an awful shame it is that Gisele can't see how Nik acts around you! But then I doubt if she's ever heard your story—'

'My story?' Olympia repeated.

'Yours and Nik's. What you were like together as teenagers. Markos told me Nik was like…totally overboard in the way he went for you…and I just couldn't *imagine* Nik like that with a woman. Since I've known him he's always been very cool and casual in the emotion department,' the redhead confessed, shaking her head in apparent wonderment. 'But around you he's a different guy…he's really intense, locked on to your every move.'

Olympia forced a smile. 'Really, Samantha…'

'No, I'm loving seeing him like this,' Samantha asserted with an only slightly guilty grin. 'Your Nik's broken plenty of hearts in his time. I'm quite transfixed, watching him surge forward to open car doors and pull out chairs for you, and you just take it *all* as your due.'

Olympia nodded without comprehension or indeed much interest. She liked Samantha, wished she had met her under other circumstances, but reckoned she would never meet her again. The day had been one of interminable strain and she could not wait for its end. Furthermore, Nik had always opened car doors and pulled out chairs for her, and she could not see anything worthy of comment in the fact. 'He has very good manners.'

Samantha sighed. 'Oh, why don't you put him out of his misery and make up with him, Olympia? I've never seen Nik as on edge as he is today.'

Olympia flushed with discomfiture. 'So it was obvious we'd had a row—'

'Oh, it wasn't you who gave it away, it was *him.*' Samantha patted Olympia's hand soothingly. 'Don't worry about it. Markos and I had several major blow-ups the first few months we were married. Getting used to living together takes time. Greek men can be incredibly bossy.'

Hands were clapping in time to the music. Olympia glanced up just as Nik was urged from his seat by their host. He shrugged out of his jacket, discarded his tie and loosened his collar before striding across the floor to join the other men.

Olympia watched the men begin to dance, the music initially sombre, the tempo slow. Nik knew every step, every turn. He was as at home dancing shoulder to shoulder with fishermen in a taverna as he was talking business on board his fabulous yacht. A rare quality which inspired respect, but she was equally conscious of the appreciative female eyes fixed to him. Nik, with his vibrant dark looks and magnetism, the potent and inescapable sexuality of that lean, muscular body accentuated by the lithe, rhythmic grace with which he moved. And it was at that point, just as the music began almost imperceptibly to quicken, that the pain inside Olympia began to break through to the surface.

She did not believe that Nik loved Gisele Bonner. She did not even believe that Nik *needed* Gisele Bonner. But Nik had betrayed her all the same. Nik did not respect either his wife or his marriage. *You have no right to resent anything.* No, no respect there. What a fool she had been to think otherwise! She could have wept at her own eagerness to believe that

something true and real might be made of a marriage which
had only ever been a business deal! Nik had the Manoulis
empire. Nik had a wife he believed he could treat like the
dirt beneath his feet when it suited him.

He hadn't even thought to warn her about that tabloid
newspaper article which Samantha had referred to with such
naive dismissal. How could she love someone who treated
her as if she was *nothing*? How, knowing what he had done,
could she have lain under him sobbing with pleasure? Her
temples pounded as the music speeded up.

It was as if an explosion was taking place inside her. Suddenly she was being bombarded by all the images that she
had shut out in self-protection. Nik pawing that skinny
blonde tart in some South of France love-nest. That skinny
blonde tart pawing Nik with the sort of expertise he was used
to and which his wife didn't have. She felt sick to the stomach, wrenched by such violent bitter jealousy she shuddered.

The music reached a soaring crescendo and came to a sudden halt. In the outbreak of vociferous applause Olympia
stood up and turned away from the table.

'Kyria Cozakis?' It was Damianos, clutching a mobile
phone in one hand, who intercepted her on her passage to
the cloakroom. 'Nik's luggage to go out to *Aurora*?' he queried uncertainly. 'The villa staff to go off duty in the middle
of the evening? Have I got this right or has there been a
mistake?'

All colour receded from Olympia's face. 'You've got it
right.'

'But Nik has no plans—'

'I have other plans, Damianos.'

The older man gazed down at her, thunderstruck by the
only possible construction he could put on that assurance.

'I suppose you're going to go and warn him now.'

'Not in a public place, *kyria*. Forgive me...' Damianos
gathered steam, his appraisal of her set features betraying

honest if incredulous concern. 'But can you have thought of what you are doing?'

Olympia nodded jerkily.

'He will go mad...'

Olympia breathed in deep and nodded. Out of the corner of her eye, she watched Damianos walk away, shoulders and back still rigid with incredulity. He had been looking after Nik for twenty years and there was a strong paternal streak in the older man's make-up, but it had been foolish of her to worry that Damianos would interfere. He would play dumb sooner than add insult to mortal injury by revealing prior knowledge of Olympia's plans.

Markos and Samantha had already risen from the table. Working his way through the crowd, a rueful smile curving his lips, Nik reached for Olympia with a confident arm and pulled her close. 'I've been neglecting you,' he said with perfect truth, dropping a careless kiss down on the crown of her head.

A salutation of approval, she recognised with a squirming sensation that took her aback. She had not committed the heresy of trying to break in on the male bonding session. She hadn't pouted and sighed like Samantha had either. Nik was relieved and pleased. Nik, she registered as she climbed into the back of the Landcruiser with Samantha, had not a *clue* of what was coming his way.

Twenty minutes later, their guests seen off on their flight home, Olympia walked hurriedly back into the villa, her hand already digging into her handbag for the photos and the newspaper cutting. Nik was only a step in her wake...

CHAPTER NINE

AFTER an instant of hesitation, Nik slung his jacket on a chair in the hall, ebony brows rising at the absence of the usual phalanx of servants who greeted his every arrival and departure. 'Where is everybody? This place feels like the *Marie Celeste.*'

Olympia snatched in a deep breath. 'I gave the staff the rest of the night off.'

Nik frowned. 'I hope you can cook…I'm hungry.'

Olympia's grip on the photos was threatening to crumple them. 'Nik—'

'Why don't you rustle up something in the food department?' Nik qualified with a shift of a vague but expectant hand. ''I could do with a shower.'

Olympia absorbed that expressive gesture. He had the body language of a male who had never needed to enter a kitchen in his entire life and who had not the slightest conception as to what went on there. Why that should strike her as endearingly naive rather than fantastically spoilt escaped her. Why, indeed, it should make her eyes sting with tears was even more of a challenge to work out. Unless it was his descent to the prosaic when she herself was wired to the skies with an impending sense of doom and drama.

One lean hand already resting on the balustrade of the staircase, Nik glanced back at Olympia, where she stood still and graven as a status. 'Olympia?'

'There's no point in you going upstairs!' Olympia exclaimed abruptly. 'I've had all your clothes packed up and sent out to *Aurora!*'

'Have you gone crazy?' Nik enquired slowly, his bemusement patent.

'No, I haven't gone crazy,' Olympia said tautly. 'I got these this morning...'

Nik studied her outstretched hand with puzzled brows.

'And if you still think that my reserved manner was sufficient to embarrass you in front of your friends, you should be feeling like a very lucky guy right now,' Olympia informed him tremulously.

Nik gave her a withering look and still made no attempt to move forward and investigate what she was holding in her hand. In fact he was making a decided point of not even looking in that direction. 'But I sense I'm *not* going to be a lucky guy as we speak,' he derided with lashings of cutting cool. 'I also see that you were being less than honest earlier when you refused to admit that there was something wrong. But I still intend to have a shower, Olympia.'

'A *shower*?' Olympia echoed in a strangled undertone.

'And that gives you fifteen minutes max to get my clothes back off *Aurora*, because I want to change,' Nik extended gently. 'Or there's going to be a hell of a row.'

In sheer disbelief, Olympia watched Nik mount the stairs. Then frustration galvanised her frozen muscles into action and she sped upstairs as well, hurrying past him to reach the landing first.

'I am sure there's a very good reason why you're acting like a child desperate to throw a tantrum in my face—'

'Don't you send me up!' Olympia seethed as rage came to her rescue. She slung the crumpled photos and the newspaper cutting at his feet. '*There!* You and your bunny-boiler! Now do you get the picture?'

'Bunny-boiler?' Nik repeated, deigning to glance down in the direction of the photos, only one of which had landed the right way up on the carpet, but not deigning to stoop to pick them up. 'What are you talking about?'

And Olympia hit him. She didn't plan to; she didn't think about it. Consumed by a head-spinning surge of rage, she clenched her fists and struck out wildly at him, connecting with his shoulder and his chest. So unprepared was Nik for that sudden attack that he almost over-balanced, and had to make a frantic grab for the banister to steady himself. Then he strode up on to the landing, snapped strong hands over her wrists and held her back from him, outrage blazing in his eyes.

'*Christos!* Are you out of your mind?' he launched at her rawly. 'What does who I slept with before our marriage have to do with you?'

Shaking like a leaf in that firm hold, Olympia gritted her teeth, shocked at herself, shocked at the fact that she wasn't getting the reaction she had expected to get. He was acting as if she was nuts and he was innocent. 'You were with her the week after our wedding!'

Without making any response, Nik released her and crouched down to gather up the photos and the cutting, treating only the second photo, which had not appeared in print, to a proper appraisal. He sprang back up again. 'Where the hell did you get these photos from?'

'The bunny-boiler.'

'The only female acting like a bunny-boiler is you,' Nik delineated with chilling cool. 'Now, take a big, deep calming breath and tell me how you got hold of these photos.'

'You're not going to talk your way out of this, Nik,' Olympia swore with quivering vehemence, and she went on to describe the message on the mirror and the magazine article which had been awaiting her in her state room on *Aurora* on their wedding day.

'And the photos?' Nik prompted, steady as a rock, but the line of his well-shaped mouth was forbidding and hard, his strong bone structure fiercely delineated beneath his bronzed skin, his increasing anger tangible.

'Planted in my handbag.'

Nik crunched the photos in a gesture of pure contemptuous dismissal and let them fall to the carpet again. Swinging on his heel, he strode downstairs with the speed and determination of a man who now had a purpose.

Both white-knuckled hands grasping the landing banister, Olympia watched him snatch his mobile phone from the pocket of his jacket, stab out a number and then start talking in Greek.

'*What* were you doing on the phone?' she demanded, when he finally slung the mobile aside again.

'Damianos will deal with this sleazy invasion of our privacy and identify the culprit,' Nik imparted with whip-like clarity, staring up at her with a thunderous frown. 'You should have told me about this immediately! That *any* employee of mine should have the insolence to play a part in such disgusting behaviour outrages me! I am not surprised that you are out of your head with…distress.'

'I'm not distressed, Nik…I'm so angry—'

'You can't punch straight…I got the message. You're very Greek when you're angry, Olympia.' Breathing in deep on that sentiment, Nik sent her a gleaming look of grim amusement. 'And as I can understand that this unpleasant campaign has been working on your mind, I can excuse your loss of control, and indeed marvel at your ability to remain even *polite* in my radius today.'

'Do you think talking all round the real issue here is going to deflect me?' Olympia demanded, her wrath and confusion only rising to ever more dangerous heights at the lowering suspicion that she was being patronised. 'Do you think I'm stupid or something?'

'These photos were taken well over a year ago,' Nik murmured very drily. 'Unfortunately the first I knew of their existence was when that tabloid chose to publish one of them. I was *not* with another woman that week. And, with regard to that offensive newspaper story, a retraction and a humble apology has since appeared in print. If I chose to discuss the matter with my lawyers rather than with you, put it down to my consideration for your feelings.'

'My feelings?' Olympia squeezed out shakily.

'I didn't want you to feel that you had been humiliated by a sleazy rag that calls itself a newspaper! I will tell you something else too,' Nik continued with a preoccupied frown. 'I can't see Gisele as the instigator of all this.'

Olympia looked unsurprised by his defence of the other woman. 'Naturally not.'

'I tell you…she's not the type. Gisele is not spiteful and we parted on good terms. Yet who *else* would have reason to target you like this?' Nik questioned for himself, mollifying Olympia slightly with that concession.

'Katerina…' Olympia suggested, unable to withhold the suggestion.

Nik's mouth compressed. 'Don't be ridiculous!'

Silence fell. Having now explained himself to his own satisfaction, Nik dealt Olympia an expectant appraisal.

A laugh with a ragged edge was torn from Olympia. 'Yes, you do think I'm stupid, don't you?'

Nik frowned. 'I've just about had enough of this, Olympia. Naturally I can produce the retraction and apology which were printed. I was *not* with Gisele the week after our wedding!'

Olympia was unimpressed. 'So you say. But you could've bribed the photographer to say he'd lied about *where* he took that photograph. You could have intimidated the newspaper editor with the threat of a big costly court case. Maybe that one photo they printed was the *only* proof they had and, let's face it, photos don't carry dates! Without further supporting evidence that you had been with Gisele, what could the newspaper do but cave in to your threats?'

'You're accusing me of lying…'

The way Nik stared at her, he couldn't seem to credit that she could dare.

'You warned me that you would do whatever you liked when you married me,' Olympia reminded him flatly.

'If I was doing what I liked right now you would be down

at my feet begging me for forgiveness!' Nik exploded with an abruptness that shook her. 'How *dare* you doubt my word?'

'Being caught out once is careless...being caught out twice is one hundred per cent proof that you're a womaniser as far as I'm concerned,' Olympia informed him fiercely. 'And I have no intention of living with a womaniser!'

Nik strode back towards the stairs. '*Twice?* Where the hell does that come from?'

'I was foolish enough to swallow your story about someone having spiked your drink ten years ago in that nightclub...but don't ask me to swallow another dose of the same nonsense where that flat-chested bunny-boiler is concerned!' Olympia spelt out bitterly.

'You are linking this peculiar business with Gisele back to—?'

'Why so incredulous, Nik? You couldn't even believe me once...you took everybody's word over mine about Lukas,' she reminded him in a voice that trembled with the force of her resentment and pain. 'If I was accused of the *same* thing again you would slaughter me where I stood and you wouldn't listen to any explanation I tried to give!'

'So we're back to squabbling over what did or did not happen in that bloody car park...I don't believe this!' Nik thrust long fingers through his luxuriant black hair, smouldering eyes fixed to her in dark, disbelieving fury.

'I don't trust you because you don't trust me. I don't trust you because we don't have a marriage; we have a business deal—'

'You shut up and you listen to me...' Nik broke in with barely leashed savagery.

Olympia shook her dark head. 'I've fulfilled my part of the deal.'

Nik threw both his arms wide apart in dark fury. 'If you use that word ''deal'' just *one* more time—'

'I'm pregnant, and now I want you to get out of this house and leave me alone.'

Nik froze, his stunning dark-as-night eyes flying to her pale frozen face and staying there for long, timeless moments. 'You're pregnant?' he echoed in open disconcertion and doubt. *'Already?'*

'Well, you put in a lot of overtime on the project, didn't you?' Olympia shivered with loathing and hurt, chilled to the bone.

Nik was appraising her with eyes that had turned dark liquid gold. 'You're so strung up you barely know what you're saying. *Theos mou*...you're pregnant,' he said again, still in shock from that revelation but beginning to show a growing sense of male satisfaction. 'You crazy, foolish woman, you could have hurt yourself hitting me!'

Olympia blinked in disconcertion.

Nik bent and lifted her off her feet with strong and very careful hands. 'You shouldn't be throwing scenes like this either. You need to lie down and stay calm...think of the baby,' he urged, taking advantage of her complete bewilderment at this sudden change in tack to stride down the corridor towards their bedroom.

'Nik...I just asked you to leave this house *and* me.'

'You don't mean it.'

'I do mean it!'

With a heavy sigh, Nik settled her down on the bed. 'You're hysterical.'

Olympia thrust her hands beneath her and reared up off the pillows. 'I am not hysterical!' she shrieked at him full blast.

'I'm not going to argue with you about this. Naturally you're upset. You're feeling suspicious and with good reason. You're right. Gisele was obviously a secret bunny-boiler who fooled me,' Nik conceded, spreading soothing hands, his calm, his control, his lack of anger now hitting her with striking effect.

'You think you've got me where you want me because I'm pregnant!' Olympia launched at him. 'Well, you haven't! My grandfather will look after my mother, so you can't get me on that, and if you don't get out of this house I'm going to take off in your yacht!'

'The crew are on leave…it would be difficult for anybody to take off anywhere in *Aurora* right now. Only the helicopter is available.'

Olympia trembled. 'You've got no right to do anything more to me than you have already done—'

'I hate to descend to this level…but if you feel like that, why did you let me make love to you this afternoon?' Nik angled a cool, enquiring scrutiny at her.

Her face burned as red as fire. 'That was sex. I *used* you because I felt like it!'

His ridiculously long black lashes lowered. He averted his head, stiffened his shoulders.

'You think that's funny, don't you? I bet you think I'm crazy about you and that this is just a lot of empty shouting and threatening…but it's not. Do you really imagine that I could be foolish enough to *care* in any way for a guy who married me just so that he get hold of my grandfather's money?'

Nik's proud head came up fast. If he had been trying to stifle amusement, he wasn't now.

'You're a laugh…you're a real laugh,' Olympia condemned with ferocious bitterness. 'So superior in every way, and yet you were willing to marry a woman you think of as a *tramp* to gain Manoulis Industries!'

Momentarily, Nik was immobile. Pallor was spreading round his rigid mouth. His eyes glittered like ice, his distaste palpable. The temperature had dropped to freezing point. Without another word, he swung on his heel and strode out of the room.

'And don't come back!' Olympia shouted after him, her voice breaking.

She sat there hunched on the bed, listening to the silence. Her eyes shimmered with tears and the blankness of shock, her emotional turmoil getting worse rather than abating. Just suppose he was telling the truth about Gisele? She crushed out that traitorous voice and hugged herself. If Nik wouldn't trust her, how could she trust him? Why, though, had he no longer been content to hear their marriage termed a 'deal'?

He had had four weeks to tell her that he wanted something more. He *hadn't*. Not a single word in that line had escaped him. She had her pride to think about. Her nose tickled, her throat closing over with tears. Pride was all she had left now that she was carrying Nik's baby. He had hurt her very badly ten years ago. She wasn't going to be hurt like that again. So she was hurting now, but by breakfast time tomorrow, after she had had a good long sleep, she would be feeling much better.

Nik's kid brother, Peri, flew in five days later.

'Hi, Peri...' Olympia said with a wobbly smile as she showed him into the impressive lounge with its spectacular vaulted ceiling.

Peri studied her shadowed, swollen eyes and her red-tipped nose. His level brown gaze was rueful. 'You're not looking good, Olly. You'd know I was lying if I said otherwise.'

To her horror, the tickly sensation of threatening tears made itself felt. She swallowed and gulped.

'Nik's not crying...but his temper's on a hair trigger and everybody with freedom of choice is staying well out of his way.'

'Where is he?'

'Athens—working, using his own apartment. My mother implied that your marriage had been a mistake,' Peri volunteered wryly. 'Nik shouted at her for the first time in his life. Then my father tried to defend my mother and I swear that Nik came within inches of hitting him. So if you're not happy, Olly...do try to remember that you're not the only

member of this family suffering. We don't usually have
punch-ups at the dinner table!'

'It's not my fault that it didn't work out,' Olympia muttered, very much on the defensive.

'May I sit down, or do I belong to the enemy camp now?'

Olympia flushed and remembered her manners. 'Of course
you can sit down. Would you like something to drink?'

'No, thanks. Just give me five minutes of your time,' Peri
urged. 'Nik doesn't know I'm here, and if he did know, he'd
rip my head off!'

'I can't discuss Nik with you. It wouldn't feel right.'

'But you can listen, can't you? Did that filthy blurb in the
papers the week after your wedding cause all this trouble
between you and my brother? You nod or you shake your
head, Olly,' Peri told her. 'That is *not* discussing Nik.'

Olympia stiffened, and then both nodded and shook her
head.

'How am I supposed to read that?' Peri groaned.

Olympia shrugged, determined not to be drawn. She was
desperate to confide in somebody, but it wouldn't be fair to
use Peri. Her sense of fairness prevented her from telling
tales of Nik to his kid brother.

'OK…Nik spent the first five days he was away from you
getting drunk as a skunk in a rented chalet in Switzerland.'
As Olympia's sea-jade eyes opened very wide, Peri added,
'I discovered he'd taken time out from your honeymoon quite
accidentally. The minute that tabloid story broke I tried to
contact Nik to warn him, and then found out that I couldn't
get hold of him. Being the really nosy guy I am, I didn't let
up until I tracked him down. He wasn't very happy to be
found.'

'I expect not drunk…*alone*?'

'Oh, no, Nik never gets to be alone, not with Damianos
around. And Damianos very much disapproves of alcohol, so
as you can imagine the atmosphere in Switzerland was not
one of companionable insobriety. Nik was getting drunk and

Damianos was pouring black coffee down him with punitive regularity.'

'Why was he getting drunk?' Olympia prompted shakily.

'He had some "stuff to work out"…that's a direct quote from Nik.'

'I got the same.' Her shoulders slumped. 'Why Switzerland?'

'Not many places you can hole up when you're supposed to be on your honeymoon and are very newsworthy. I don't think Nik saw the alpine pastures except through an alcoholic haze.'

Silence stretched. Peri looked at Olympia. Olympia looked hopefully at Peri.

'He sobered up into a rage when I told him about that gutter press article. He spent the last day sorting that out with his lawyers. At no stage was he in a position to enjoy a lusty poolside clinch with Gisele…' Peri's mouth quirked. 'In fact I doubt he'll enjoy a lusty clinch outdoors ever again now that that photo's come back to haunt him. It would make *me* think twice, I can tell you!'

Olympia reddened. 'You'd lie for Nik—'

'If he had been with Gisele, I'd take the view that it was none of my business and you were better off out of it.'

Olympia chewed at her lower lip. 'Nik's a womaniser.'

'Well, before you came along ten years ago, *yes*…after you broke up, *yes*…but never when you were around. Not at present either!' Peri hastened to assure her.

The tears welled up and rolled down her cheeks. 'It's not that I don't appreciate what you're trying to do, Peri,' Olympia admitted chokily. 'I do, but it's too late for Nik and me. Something rotten happened a long time ago and it's always going to be there between us and it can't be fixed. I *made* Nik go…I practically threw him out and I deliberately said what I knew would drive him away.'

Emanating intense curiosity, Peri studied her with anticipation.

'I'm not saying any more. I've said too much already. Will you stay for dinner?' she asked hopefully, because she was so lonely.

'Sorry. If I don't want Nik to ask where I've been, I need to get back.' Peri rose upright.

Olympia stretched up and kissed his cheek, loving him for trying to help. 'You're so different from Nik.'

'I was the unexpected baby when my parents had given up all hope of the patter of tiny feet sounding again. I was *ruined*!' Peri emphasised.

'Wasn't Nik?'

'No. Nik was told to act like a *man* when he was scared of the dark as a kid. I got an open door, a night light, and my father held my hand and told me an extra story,' Peri reeled off with a comical grimace. 'Nik got sent to a military academy where a rigorous macho regime of cold showers and assault courses was aimed at honing his competitive instincts to a killing edge! I doubt if he got much encouragement to share his deepest feelings there.'

'Where did you go to school?' Olympia was fascinated.

'A mile from home and I never boarded. I burst into tears when they mentioned the academy and it was never mentioned again.'

Peri left Olympia with a lot to consider. Even the most suspicious wife would have been challenged to continue believing that Nik had been unfaithful. Olympia had been challenged to believe that even *before* Peri arrived.

Nik had not shown a hint of guilt or discomfiture when she'd accused him of being with Gisele. Nik had just been furious. All he had cared about was finding out how she had got hold of those wretched photos and ensuring that the culprit who had aided his former mistress in her campaign was identified. And the oddest thing was that Olympia was no longer even sure that she had *ever* really believed at heart that Nik had been unfaithful.

It was as though her mounting resentment at Nik's refusal

to listen to her explanation about Katerina and Lukas had destroyed her usual common sense. She had also been feeling increasingly insecure. Yes, she had been very, very happy with Nik during their weeks on *Aurora*, but underneath there had always been the sinking awareness that Nik had not actually *said* anything to reassure her that he had overcome his medieval desire to avenge his honour.

And somehow…in retrospect, she didn't really know *how*…her emotions had just taken over and everything had mushroomed out of all proportion. So she had got rid of him. And the minute Nik had gone out of the door, loweringly, she had wanted him back, but had been too stubborn and proud to admit it. She had spent the night telling herself that she had done the right thing and the early hours worrying that she had been too hasty in throwing him out. She had spent breakfast weeping like a wimp over the acknowledgement that Nik had positively glowed like a proud father-to-be once he had realised that she was pregnant.

But, ironically, Olympia was most upset by something which Peri had dropped quite casually: if Alexandra Cozakis had commented that their marriage had been a mistake, Nik had evidently informed his parents that their marriage was in trouble. Announcing that to the wider family circle seemed so final, so horribly, immovably final. Was Nik thinking about a divorce now?

Olympia was still keeping in touch with her own mother on an almost daily basis, and going to enormous lengths not to lie but not to tell the whole truth either! Irini Manoulis was currently living outside Athens with Olympia's grandfather, and naturally awaiting some kind of invitation from her newly married daughter. Olympia had been reduced to saying that Nik was away on business and that she was incredibly busy…

The phone was brought to her at two that afternoon. Expecting the caller to be her mother, Olympia answered in a bright upbeat tone. 'Mum?'

'It's Nik.'

He didn't sound like himself. He sounded flat, taut, expressionless.

'Are you all right?' she pressed instantly.

Silence sizzled on the line.

Olympia was holding the phone so tight she was hurting her fingers. She had just heard his voice and all pride and self-discipline had vanished. She was thinking of crawling, and hating herself for it. 'Maybe you think that in the light of what I said and did that is a funny thing for me to ask,' she began, hoping to draw out the dialogue as long as possible—which meant she had to do all the talking because it didn't sound as if *he* was going to be much help in that field.

'I'm *not* all right,' Nik informed her. 'Look, the helicopter will bring you to Athens for eight. I'll see you then.'

'Nik?'

'What?'

She breathed in jaggedly, eyes ready to overflow again. 'I'm just so miserable!'

'You got what you wanted. You got my favourite house. You got my baby. You haven't got me,' Nik enumerated curtly.

'But I *want* you!' Olympia sobbed, before she could swallow that despairing cry back again.

The silence stretched and stretched like a giant elastic band attached to her sensitive nerve-endings. At any moment she expected it to snap and rip her down the middle.

She heard Nik clear his throat, but he still said nothing.

'I just don't know what to say,' he finally advanced gruffly when she had practically given up all hope of a response.

'Fine...don't worry about it...I know I shan't!' In a flood of tears, she stuffed the phone under two cushions, listening to it ring and ring and ignoring it. The roof had fallen in on her just as Nik had always forecast. Reckless to the point of self-destruction. He'd been right. She had trashed the relationship they had built up. If there had ever been any hope of them staying together she had destroyed that hope all on her own. And it was going to be precious little comfort to her in the future that she had held on to her principles. Already loving Nik, needing Nik, was starting to feel like a life sentence of craving what she couldn't have.

The housekeeper entered the lounge with a gentle knock on the door and another phone. Olympia accepted it with writhing reluctance.

'Olympia?' Nik grated rawly.

'I'll see you at eight. I only said I wanted you because of the baby!' Olympia lied, and after a couple of seconds the phone went dead.

So they would discuss their divorce, or their separation. No, the lawyers would see to the technicalities. Why had she lied like that about the baby? Nik hadn't deserved to be insulted again just so that she could save face.

Olympia dressed in unrelieved black to fly to Athens. A stretch limo ferried her through the busy streets at a snail's pace. There was plenty of time for her to ponder her mistakes and her misery and she didn't bother looking out of the window. So when the limo finally drew to a halt, and she climbed out to gaze up at the huge stone mansion in front of her, it was a horrible shock to realise that she had been brought to the Cozakis *family* home, rather than Nik's apartment or even his office.

A very correct manservant ushered her into the classical hall with its chilly but impressive decor and sculptured heads set on plinths. Olympia could feel herself dwindling in stature right back down into the nervous and intimidated teenager whom Nik had brought home to meet his parents. She had tried to edge back out through the door again, muttering that maybe it was a bit too soon for such a meeting, and Nik had yanked her back.

Momentarily, her eyes shimmered with tears over the memory. For a crazy instant she wanted to be transported back into her seventeen-year-old self, strengthened with all the knowledge she had acquired since their marriage. Most of all, she wanted to experience just once what she had been far too insecure to recognise then…that Nik had truly *loved* her.

'Olympia…'

She jerked round. Nik was in a doorway staring at her. She stopped breathing. Her heart just jumped and raced. She connected with his spectacular gaze, those jaguar-gold eyes surrounded by inky black lashes. She went weak at the knees. Her attention expanded to rove all over him. The bold, dark features, the intrinsic aura of intense maleness which made breathing such a challenge, the palest grey suit exquisitely tailored to his magnificent athletic physique.

'All four limbs still present and correct, head better screwed on…' Nik muttered tautly.

She didn't know what he was talking about. She didn't *care*. She just walked across the hall as if he had yanked on a string.

'There's only a few things I need to say to you…'

She froze, stricken eyes veiling. 'Better keep the limo waiting, then.'

How had she missed out on noticing straight off how much strain Nik was betraying? It was etched in the clean, tight lines of his bone structure and the set of his mouth. He had lost weight since she had last seen him and he was pale.

He showed her into a book-lined room. 'Firstly, I've torn up all the copies of that offensive pre-marital contract I made you sign.'

Olympia was not noticeably cheered by that announcement. He was feeling guilty, she thought. He was now willing to offer generous financial compensation in place of himself. She was obviously going to be a *rich* ex-wife.

Nik reached for her hand. 'You accused me of marrying you for what I would gain. I asked for that by not telling you the truth about the deal I made with Spyros. I may *control* your grandfather's business empire but he still *owns* it and can still dispose of it as he wishes.'

Olympia was astonished by that admission. 'But—'

'Spyros didn't want it that way but I insisted. At the time, I assumed that our marriage would end in divorce,' Nik completed heavily.

That made a great deal of sense to Olympia. Nik had wanted revenge more than he'd wanted profit. It had also suited him to let her believe that she was wholly dependent on him for security. Furthermore, when their marriage broke up, her grandfather could not feel cheated for he would have lost nothing by such an agreement.

Olympia was now paper-pale. Nik was dealing with all the remaining sources of resentment and misunderstanding that still lay between them.

'One last point...without doubt the most important point...' Nik hesitated.

The baby. Access arrangements? The necessity of maintaining a civil relationship in spite of their no longer living together? Her throat convulsed.

'It took me a long time to learn what should have been a very simple lesson,' Nik confided with driven urgency. 'Lukas? That was nothing—indeed, when set against more important matters, a complete triviality.'

'A c-complete triviality?' Olympia stammered with sheer incredulity.

'You saw me in the arms of an ex-girlfriend...*you hit back*. At least that's how I saw it then, and it made complete sense at the time to me,' Nik spelt out in a charged, almost bitter undertone. 'I had you on this pure, perfect pedestal, and when you seemed to jump off it I was gutted. I carried that feeling for ten years, nourished it, hated you beyond all reason—'

'I understand,' she broke in, lowering her head wearily even as something in his wording nagged at the back of her mind. 'I felt the same way about you.'

'And when it came to Lukas and you,' Nik continued tautly. 'When it came to trying to deal with that here, in the present, I was still frozen in time at the age of nineteen. So I reacted like a boy, *not* like a man. I need you to understand that.'

Olympia's head was spinning. Nik was being so open, so honest. He seemed to be trying to prove that he had finally forgiven her for what she hadn't actually done. He was even attempting to foist some of the blame for the episode on himself. He was offering an unconditional acceptance of both her and the past which she had never expected to receive. And then what had nagged at her in Nik's wording a minute earlier was clarified. 'You *seemed* to jump off...it made complete sense *at the time*...' Nik was talking as though he now doubted her guilt.

'You said you wanted me...' Nik breathed roughly, throwing her thoughts into confusion again. *'Back?'*

Olympia's sea-jade eyes connected with dark golden eyes. His tension was strong as her own. 'Back,' she confirmed instantaneously.

Nik released his breath audibly and closed both arms tightly round her. She could feel his heart going thump-thump-thump against her as if he had just run a marathon. Slowly he lifted his proud dark head. The look of intense strain was back in his taut gaze. He lifted his hands to her face, curving his fingers round her cheekbones.

'Katerina is here,' he told her then, startling her.

'Katerina?'

'Spyros is here as well.'

'My grandfather?' Olympia was in shock at those twin announcements.

'With the obvious exception of Lukas, I have assembled everybody who was originally involved in our broken engagement ten years ago,' Nik advanced as he walked her back into the hall and towards the drawing room. 'They have

all simply had dinner together and your arrival will be unexpected. That is how I planned it.'

'Planned it?' she questioned, but Nik was already opening
the door and standing back for her entrance.

CHAPTER TEN

FIVE heads turned towards the door, and with only two exceptions all faces betrayed discomfiture of varying degrees when Olympia appeared.

Spyros Manoulis looked the least surprised and the most pleased. Nik's brother, Peri, greeted her with a wide grin of approval. Achilles, Nik's father, who always looked forbidding, merely stiffened. Nik's mother, Alexandra, cosily seated beside Katerina, froze with unease. And Katerina? Katerina stared, and then pinned a bright smile to her lips.

The other woman had no fear, either of Olympia or of her lies being exposed, Olympia recognised bitterly. In pleased receipt of a warm hug from her grandfather, and a cooler acknowledgement of her arrival from the other parties present, she took a seat. How was she supposed to confront Katerina without any proof that she had lied? Why should Nik's cousin confess anything when she had so much to lose? While Olympia was frantically wondering what she could say that might provoke the brunette into showing her true colours, Nik started talking.

'I have a story to tell you all,' Nik drawled lazily from his stance by the marble fireplace.

Curiosity awakened, everybody sat up a little straighter to listen. But when Olympia realised what story it was that Nik intended to tell she was disconcerted and embarrassed. She decided that the minute she got him out of the room she would kill him! It was purgatory to be forced to sit there while Nik told the tale of the message on the mirror on their wedding night, and then went on to mention the newspaper article which he had tried to protect Olympia from. By the time he got round to the photos which she had found hidden in her handbag Olympia was squirming.

Achilles Cozakis breathed with distaste. 'A most unpleasant business.'

Alexandra Cozakis, who had turned to ice at the mere mention of her eldest son featuring in an intimate photograph with Gisele Bonner, said without hesitation, 'That was the behaviour of a very malicious woman.'

'Disgraceful!' Spyros Manoulis pronounced, with sincere annoyance on his granddaughter's behalf.

'Now I know why I never really took to Gisele,' Peri mused with a grimace.

'How *awful* for you!' Katerina gasped in turn, giving Olympia a look of caring commiseration.

Katerina's exclamation seemed to draw everybody's attention to the fact that neither of Nik's parents had offered their daughter-in-law sympathy for what she had suffered.

'Who do you think was behind that campaign against my wife?' Nik enquired softly.

Everybody frowned while they tried to work out why he was asking what appeared to be a stupid question.

'It *wasn't* Gisele,' Nik emphasised, and he drew a folded document from the inside pocket of his jacket. 'It was a member of this family. Someone who has run tame in this house since I was a child. Someone we trust, someone we care about.'

Comprehension hit Olympia as she looked across the room and recognised that Katerina had turned as white as milk. The brunette was sitting forward on her seat, her tension palpable. Dear heaven, Olympia realised then. It hadn't been Gisele behind that campaign; it had been Katerina!

'You shouldn't have been so careless, Katerina. Damianos is a very thorough investigator,' Nik delivered.

The whole room seemed to erupt then. Nik's parents spoke up in furious Greek, most probably defending Katerina, who had burst into instant floods of tears.

'Use English,' Nik cut in with quiet authority. 'Olympia's Greek is much improved, but you are speaking too quickly and nobody has a greater right to understand all that is said here. And before anybody gets carried away with the need to comfort my cousin, let me tell you how she contrived to wage such a campaign.'

Katerina had been on board *Aurora* with Achilles and Alexandra Cozakis the week before the wedding. She had bribed Olympia's maid into carrying out her instructions. Nik handed the document in his hand to his father. 'The maid was in regular contact with Katerina during our honeymoon. Katerina flew to Spain to meet up with the maid and pass over the photos. That meeting was witnessed by another crew member. The photographer who sold the photos to Katerina was willing to identify her. The evidence against my cousin is incontrovertible.'

'How could you imagine that I would do such dreadful things?' Katerina wept brokenly.

'Because it wasn't the first time, was it?' Olympia heard herself answer, and slowly she rose to her feet.

'What's that supposed to mean?' the brunette demanded, her voice stronger the instant she saw Olympia in front of her, her hostility unconcealed.

'When Nik and I got engaged ten years ago, you decided to break us up.'

'I have no idea what you're talking about,' Katerina said woodenly.

'Like hell you haven't!' Nik launched without warning at his cousin. 'Ten years ago you *swore* in front of witnesses that you caught Lukas and Olympia having sex in my car!'

Such plain speaking provoked a moan of reproof from Nik's already shaken mother.

'I'm sorry.' Olympia was sympathetic towards the older woman's embarrassment. 'Of course you don't want to be forced to listen to anything more unpleasant, but this does have to be cleared up. I was unjustly accused and I do want the truth to be known and accepted.'

'Katerina!' Nik thundered impatiently.

'All right!' Katerina said flatly. 'For what its worth, I got together with Lukas and we set you both up. Nothing happened between Lukas and Olympia...I just made the whole story up! Are you satisfied now?'

An unearthly silence fell at that unemotional rendering of such offensive facts.

'*Why?* Nik demanded with sudden rawness. 'Why would you make such filthy allegations about my fiancé? You're my cousin. Lukas was my friend.'

Katerina turned her head away in mute refusal to respond. In silence, Spyros Manoulis ushered Olympia back into her seat and remained beside her.

'She was in love with you, Nik,' Olympia sighed ruefully. 'I'm afraid it was a little more than just a crush. I moved in on what she saw as her territory and she's hated me for that ever since.'

'I am appalled by this,' Achilles Cozakis admitted to Olympia, making no attempt to conceal his horrified embarrassment at the lies which the brunette had told. 'We accepted everything Katerina said without question.'

'I too am filled with disgust, Katerina,' Alexandra Cozakis stated with tear-filled eyes but a cold, steady voice. 'You hurt and distressed my son and destroyed Olympia's good reputation. Yet I remember how warmly Olympia received your offer of friendship. She did you no harm and neither did Nik. Your lack of shame even now shocks me most.'

Beneath that onslaught of censure, Katerina's face hardened.

'What was Lukas's part in all this?' Nik breathed with a roughened edge to his dark drawl, ashen pale now beneath his bronzed skin.

'Lukas had to get very drunk to do what he did that night, Nik,' Olympia answered in gentle consolation. 'He was very unhappy about it, but he seemed to believe that if the Cozakis and Manoulis families got together in business, his family's company would be unable to compete.'

Nik awarded Olympia a stunned look of comprehension. 'Yes, when I think of it, that *would* have been a possibility, but it did not occur to any of us at the time. *Christos*...where were my wits?'

'We can be grateful that at least Lukas's parents don't have to live with the knowledge of their dead son's part in this sordid affair,' Achilles Cozakis stepped in to say, his tone one of finality before he turned to address Katerina. 'I have called a car for you. You will not be welcome in this house again!'

'You were *still* telling lies about Olympia on our wedding day!' Nik suddenly erupted in an outraged roar, taking everybody by surprise.

Katerina jumped up, her face twisting with sudden fury and violent resentment as she stalked to the door. 'You could have had me as a wife but you picked a nothing, a bastard from a backstreet in London, and you got what you deserved!'

Nik's parents reared back in almost comical horror from Katerina's rage and abuse. It was clear that neither had ever seen that side of the younger woman.

'No, Olympia got what I deserved,' Nik muttered with sick distaste, and turned away as the door slammed on his cousin's exit.

'What a *lively* family you have, Achilles!' Spyros Manoulis said to Nik's father in apparent wonderment. 'But that one who has just gone out is a snake. I would not like to think that Katerina would again be in a position where she might harm Olympia.'

'She leapt up like a madwoman!' Alexandra Cozakis gasped with a stricken sob. 'Who would ever have thought that Katerina could be like that?'

'Be assured that that young woman will cause no further

trouble,' Achilles Cozakis asserted in considerable mortification, patting his distraught wife's shoulder. 'But I think we have all had enough of her for one evening.'

Nik was by the window, silent, still, and not looking in anybody's direction.

'Yes, indeed.' Spyros extended a hand down to Olympia, who clasped it and stood up. 'By the way, I'm taking my granddaughter home with me.'

'Home with you...' Olympia echoed, thunderstruck by that casual announcement.

Nik seemed to emerge from his abstraction. Swinging round, he took an almost clumsy step forward, as totally taken aback by that development as everybody else. 'What are you saying, Spyros?'

'I'm taking her back. You don't deserve her. In my home she will be properly valued and protected.'

'Spyros...Nik is in shock, as we all are,' Achilles Cozakis intervened in dismay. 'We are *all* very much aware that amends must be made to Olympia for her treatment, not only in the past but in the present. We are painfully conscious of our mistakes and prejudices.'

'Come on, Olympia...' Olympia found herself being hustled towards the door at speed by her determined grandfather, who paused in the doorway only to say in conclusion, 'You have lost yourself a fine woman, Nik Cozakis!'

'That'll give my son-in-law something more sensible to worry about!' Spyros chuckled as he swept them both out of the Cozakis mansion. 'Did you see their faces? All that weeping and wailing! We Manoulises are people of action.'

'But I don't want to leave Nik,' Olympia protested shakily, the evening's events beginning to catch up with her as well, leaving her feeling momentarily weak and weepy and out of touch with what was happening around her.

'I know what I'm doing.' Her grandfather urged her with gentle hands into the limo waiting outside. 'I'm stealing you back for an hour. Now that you're married, Nik's welcome to spend the night in my home.'

'How can he spend the night when he's not with us?'

'Olympia…tonight Nik was so weighed down with his guilt and his bitterness he was in a stupor, and I felt sorry for him. When he saw his wife being trailed away, he went from the stupor into panic…much more healthy!' Spyros asserted, patting her tightly linked hands in a comforting gesture. 'I have no doubt that Nik will be pounding my front door long before midnight! However, I also cruelly misjudged you, and we *also* have fences to mend.'

And Olympia and her grandfather did mend those fences, quite happily, and, being both of a blunt disposition, they did the mending within a very few words. Had Olympia had Nik by her side she would have felt happier; she did not have her grandfather's faith in the belief that Nik would immediately chase after her.

Arriving at Spyros's villa, she was engulfed in a rapturous welcome by her mother, who was looking terrific.

'Doesn't she look well?' Spyros said proudly of his daughter, Irini. 'Good Greek air performed the miracle.'

Neither Olympia nor her grandfather saw any point in distressing Irini Manoulis with the evening's events. Olympia chose to share the news of her pregnancy instead. Spyros was ecstatic, and broke out a bottle of champagne. Her mother glowed with excitement and briefly wondered where Nik was.

'You'll see Nik over the breakfast table,' Spyros promised, ignoring Olympia's strained look.

Her mother showed her into a spacious guest room and sat down on the edge of the divan to chat to her daughter at length about babies. She began to yawn a little then, and Olympia persuaded her to go to bed. Soon after that, a loud knock sounded on the door and her grandfather appeared looking very smug. He said nothing, though. He just stepped back, and only then did Nik move into view.

His tie was missing, his black hair ruffled, half his shirt undone, a definable dark shadow now roughening his strong jawline. He was far from immaculate but, being Nik, he still contrived to look absolutely gorgeous. Her heart started beating so fast she felt as if she couldn't breathe.

The silence was too much for Spyros. He slapped Nik on the back. 'Even I didn't expect a grandchild on the way this soon!' he admitted, before mercifully closing the door to leave them alone.

Olympia was cringing with mortification.

Nik had frozen in receipt of that congratulatory slap. Haunted night-dark eyes rested on Olympia. 'I didn't give you much choice, did I?'

'I'm really pleased about the baby...' Olympia told him.

'You have to be, don't you?' Nik sighed.

'I am really happy about our baby,' Olympia repeated doggedly, recognising the strain etched in his vibrant dark features. 'Why did it take you so long to get over here?'

'The limo broke down. I had to get a cab, and then it got stuck in a traffic jam, and I ended up walking the rest of the way with Damianos grousing in my wake.'

Olympia had to gulp back a nervous laugh.

Nik swallowed. One of his hands moved in an awkward gesture and then stilled again. He watched her with intense and beautiful dark eyes and then he breathed in very deep. 'You know I love you so much it hurts...' he said with ragged sincerity.

She flew off the edge of the bed and flung herself at him.

Nik caught her into his arms and held her so close she almost couldn't breathe. 'I was planning to say a lot of other things, but when it comes down to it loving you is about the only thing I've got to offer in my favour.'

'Rubbish,' Olympia scolded chokily.

'I thought I knew so much ten years ago and I didn't know anything. I should have *known* they were lying!' Nik groaned into her hair. 'I can't forgive myself for being that stupid. How can you? I wrecked everything for us—'

'We were so young, and we were both so desperate to save face we couldn't be honest with each other.' She smoothed possessive fingers through his black hair, allowing happiness to channel through her in an exhilarating wave. 'I don't want to look back any more, Nik. You can't look out for the Katerinas of this world. She was very clever and very convincing. I really trusted her as a friend and I was shattered at the way she just turned on me that night.'

'When Damianos found the photo trail led back to her I was devastated, and I knew instantly that everything you had ever tried to tell me about her had to be true,' Nik confided tautly.

'When did you find out?'

'Late last night. My first urge was to fly straight out to Kritos, but I decided it would be better to confront Katerina and that you had the right to be there too.' His beautiful mouth tightened. 'I didn't want to tell you in advance in case in some way you alerted her and put her on her guard. I knew we didn't have a shred of proof about what she did ten years ago, but I was determined to get the truth out of her for your sake.'

'I'm so grateful you had the evidence that it was her behind those photos.'

Nik looked down at her with immense regret. 'She caused us so much misery. But there's never been anybody but you in my heart…nobody else even came close.'

Olympia hugged him tight, his gruff honesty bringing tears to her eyes.

'I really had already overcome my…my—'

'Unreasonable feelings about what you thought I had done with Lukas?' Olympia put in helpfully. 'I *know* you had. You made that quite clear—'

'The day you threw me out of the house.'

'I know.' Olympia sighed lovingly. 'You got no credit at

all. The fact sort of got lost in what I was feeling about those photos.'

'Katerina again,' Nik ground out.

Olympia snuggled past his jacket into his shirtfront, drinking in the achingly familiar scent of him, wonderfully aware of the tall, hard, lean length of him. 'Do you know she actually told me that our marriage was arranged before you even met me?'

'What nonsense is that?' Nik held her back from him.

'I know,' Olympia sighed shame-facedly. 'How could I have believed something so far-fetched?'

'There was no arranged marriage.' Nik cupped her cheekbones. His gorgeous dark eyes sought hers with glimmering amusement. 'But I did see a photo of you in Spyros's office the year before we met,' he confided. 'You were sitting with a white cat on your knee. You had such a glorious smile that I had to ask your grandfather who you were.'

Olympia stared up at him in surprise, for she recalled that photo.

'Your grandfather knew I was impressed, and that may be why he invited me over to meet you as soon as you arrived in Greece...I wouldn't put it past him.'

'Neither would I...' But Olympia smiled, tickled pink by the idea of Nik having admired her that much even before he met her. 'Were your parents feeling better by the time you left?'

'They're very upset about the way they've treated you, and concerned that they may inadvertently have encouraged Katerina. Possibly there was a time when my mother thought she wouldn't mind if I married her,' Nik acknowledged grimly. 'However, I never had the slightest interest in her in that way.'

'But she doesn't ever seem to have faced that, which is very strange.' Olympia frowned, feeling sorry for the other woman as she recognised how irrational Katerina's behaviour had been.

'Because she's obsessed. My father will talk to her family and suggest that she has professional help. It's not a problem that can be ignored. I suspect that guilt over Lukas's death may have hit Katerina harder than any of us could have appreciated,' Nik conceded ruefully. 'He was infatuated with her. How must she have felt when he crashed that car?'

Olympia shivered, and decided a change of subject was overdue. 'Tell me, would you *really* have dumped me back at my family's feet in front of our wedding guests?'

A dark flush scored Nik's fabulous cheekbones. 'I wanted you to think I would. *Christos*...the minute you forced your way into my office it all started up again for me. But it had to be on my terms this time, so that I felt I was in control. Then the minute we made love, on our wedding night, everything just went haywire for me...'

'How?'

'You were seasick and all I wanted to do was look after you.' Nik groaned. 'And then we lay talking on the bed and it felt completely right, not strange at all. It actually felt as if we'd never been apart.'

'Really?' Olympia was delighted by that admission.

'All of a sudden I couldn't kid myself that I was still in control. That's why I took off the next day.' Nik grimaced. 'I didn't like what I was feeling.'

'What were you feeling?'

Nik released a self-mocking laugh. 'If I'd known I wouldn't have had to go away. I went to Switzerland and I was absolutely bloody miserable, sitting drowning my sorrows.'

'I'm glad you were miserable because I was too. What conclusions did you come to?'

'That I was in trouble, *agape mou*. That I wanted to be with you rather than in Switzerland. That I still had feelings I didn't want to examine too closely,' Nik admitted with a rueful twist of his sensual mouth. 'And then we got together again in Spain and I didn't bother beating myself up any more about what I might or might not have been feeling.'

Olympia looked up at him in reluctant fascination and reproach.

Nik said defensively, 'I was really happy, but I know I should have mentioned that that outrageous marriage deal idea was history as far as I was concerned. But then I didn't know how you felt...'

'And no way were *you* going to say anything before *I* did...' Olympia recognised, giving him a teasing look of comprehension.

'You *still* haven't said anything,' Nik reminded her, studying her with brilliant dark eyes.

Olympia's eyes danced. 'It was your turn this time...I did all the talking ten years ago!' She stretched up on her tiptoes and linked her arms round his neck. 'I love you, Nik Cozakis...'

Liquid dark golden eyes gazed down into her. 'Madly, totally and for ever?'

'What a memory you've got!' Olympia was thrilled he could recall her saying those words to him ten years earlier. He must have treasured them to remember them so well, and that really touched her.

'That's how much I love you,' Nik confessed, bending his dark head to taste her mouth with aching slowness. Her heart sang and her knees trembled, and suddenly she was moving backwards, well aware that there was a bed behind her.

Nik came down beside her with a wolfish grin. 'We've still got talking to do...'

Olympia flicked a button loose on his shirt. 'I'm listening.'

He grasped her hand, eyes suddenly level and serious again. 'These last few days away from you were hell. I was really scared I'd lost you. When you said you wanted me back, on the phone, I felt so sick with relief I couldn't think of a thing to say.'

'Sometimes actions speak louder.' Olympia lay back

against the pillows with the faint air of a woman arranging herself to her best advantage. 'You're not great on the phone, but you have your talents in other places.'

'Picking bunny-boilers?' Nik asked with glinting eyes, shrugging out of his jacket with fluid sexy ease.

'Are you ever going to let me forget that scene I made?' She groaned, her face burning. 'I never said sorry for hitting you either.'

'And I never said sorry for going on like a jerk about the way you were acting that day. It's just I didn't know what was wrong and I was panicking.' Nik sighed and kissed her with slow, sensual intensity.

'I saw that,' she whispered tenderly.

'You won't get the chance to accuse me of straying again. I don't like being away from you. I'll cut down on travel so that we can base ourselves on the island,' Nik shared huskily, resting the palm of his hand on her still flat stomach and smiling at her with unconcealed contentment at that prospect. 'You and me and the baby together.'

It sounded like paradise to Olympia. They exchanged another kiss. It went on a little longer than the previous one. They shifted closer and closer. Nik admitted he felt very strange, getting put into a bedroom with her in her grandfather's home, and they both started laughing. And when the laughing stopped they lost themselves in each other, the experience all the more intense and all the sweeter for the love they now openly shared.

Olympia settled their infant daughter into her cradle. Alyssa had loads of dark curly hair and eyes the colour of sea jade. And from the hour of her birth she had drawn both Nik and Olympia's families closer together.

Spyros Manoulis was a regular visitor. Spyros, who had had little to do with his own children because he had been too busy building his empire while they were growing up, had succumbed to a fever of adoration for his great-granddaughter, whose every tiny move he applauded. Olympia's mother, Irini, whose health had improved in step with her increasing sense of wellbeing, was an equally keen grandmother, but currently had another interest in her life as well.

Olympia smiled at the memory of her grandfather's shock the previous winter, when his middle-aged daughter had gone out to dinner with a retired widower she had met through friends. Irini was getting married to Sotiris in a few weeks' time and Olympia was looking forward to the wedding.

Achilles and Alexandra Cozakis could not have done more than they had done over the past year to establish a close and loving relationship with their daughter-in-law. Peri's irreverent sense of humour had done much to lessen the strain which Katerina had left in her wake. And Alyssa, adored by all, had been a wonderful blessing.

About six months after that night when Katerina's lies had been exposed, Katerina had written to Nik and Olympia offering them her assurance that never again would she seek to interfere in their lives and saying that she now deeply regretted all the trouble she had caused. Since then Katerina had moved to London, to live with her elder sister and her family, and was apparently embarking on a new life.

There was not a single cloud in Olympia's world. Exactly a year ago she had married Nik, expecting nothing but hurt and pain to result, and since then she had gained the loving support of two families, a gorgeous baby daughter and a husband she loved more with every passing day. This was their wedding anniversary, but they were staying home on Kritos because with the number of social invitations they received staying home alone was more of a treat than going out.

Olympia fingered the diamond necklace round her throat and looked in the mirror with a secretive smile. Once she wouldn't have thought she suited diamonds. Then she had begun seeing herself through Nik's eyes, and finally through her own, and her old lack of confidence was long gone. Her reflection showed a woman with very long dark hair—Nik's pleas had prevailed—wearing a beautiful designer gown that made the most of her lush breasts and hips.

'Sensational…' Nik purred from the doorway.

Olympia gave a sensuous little wriggle of appreciation as he kissed one smooth bare shoulder.

Nik gazed down at their baby daughter with softened eyes. 'She's tremendous. Do you know what my first thought was when you threw me out of the house nearly a year ago?'

'I didn't know Olympia had the guts?' Olympia teased, turning round to study him, her attention roaming over his vibrant good looks with possessive appreciation and, even now, a heart which developed a distinctly rapid beat at his proximity.

'No. What if she has a boy and says, Right, that's it. You've got your son and heir, where's my divorce?' Nik confessed with a rueful groan of remembrance. 'I started praying for a whole succession of girls the same moment!'

Olympia was entranced by that admission. She liked him to know that he had almost shot himself in the foot with that marriage deal he had proposed. But as a bridge to a shared future which he couldn't have brought himself to reach for otherwise the marriage deal had worked just great, in her opinion. They had enjoyed such a blissfully happy first year together, and she had been fortunate enough to have an easy pregnancy and delivery.

Nik laced his fingers with hers and kissed her with all the considerable skill in his repertoire. 'I love you, *agape mou*.'

'Madly, totally and for ever,' she confided, quivering a little with a heat that was all too familiar and pulling herself back from him by exerting every means of self-control she knew. 'Dinner,' she reminded him, colouring.

'It was just one kiss,' Nik pointed out.

It rarely stopped at one kiss, though.

They strolled out to the stone terrace and took their seats at the beautifully set table awaiting them. In the drowsing heat of early evening, Olympia took in the magnificent views which had so enchanted her on her first morning on the island. And then she gazed at Nik, more enchanted than ever.

He was the love of her life, and on that thought she began to eat the exquisitely cooked meal which was being served to them. Their eyes met, jaguar-gold into green, with increasing frequency. And if they ate a little more quickly than was expected, and got a bit impatient between courses, and vanished altogether before the coffee arrived, the staff weren't surprised. They had seen it all so many times before.

Don't miss a fabulous new trilogy
from a rising star in

HARLEQUIN 🜀 PRESENTS®

KIM LAWRENCE

**Wanted:
three husbands
for three sisters!**

*Triplet sisters—they're
the best, the closest,
of friends...*

Meet lively, spirited Anna in
Wild and Willing!, Harlequin Presents® #2078
On sale December 1999

Lindy meets the man of her dreams in
The Secret Father, Harlequin Presents® #2096
On sale March 2000

Hope's story is the thrilling conclusion
to this fabulous trilogy in
An Innocent Affair, Harlequin Presents® #2114
On sale June 2000

Available wherever Harlequin books are sold.

HPTB1

Back by popular demand are
DEBBIE MACOMBER's

Hard Luck, Alaska, is a
town that needs women!
And the O'Halloran brothers
are just the fellows
to fly them in.

Starting in March 2000 this beloved series returns
in special 2-in-1 collector's editions:

MAIL-ORDER MARRIAGES, featuring
Brides for Brothers and *The Marriage Risk*
On sale March 2000

FAMILY MEN, featuring
Daddy's Little Helper and *Because of the Baby*
On sale July 2000

THE LAST TWO BACHELORS, featuring
Falling for Him and *Ending in Marriage*
On sale August 2000

Collect and enjoy each MIDNIGHT SONS story!

Available at your favorite retail outlet.

HARLEQUIN®
Makes any time special ™

Visit us at www.romance.net   PHMS

Coming Next Month

THE BEST HAS JUST GOTTEN BETTER!

#2109 THE MILLIONAIRE'S VIRGIN Anne Mather
Nikolas has obviously not forgiven Paige for walking out on him
four years ago. So why has he offered her a job on his Greek island
for the summer? And what exactly will he be expecting from her?

#2110 THE CATTLE KING'S MISTRESS Emma Darcy
Nathan King, powerful head of his family's cattle empire, wants
Miranda, but doubts she'll cope with outback life. Miranda wants
Nathan, too, but believes her past will deny her the chance of a
future with a King. Yet the passion between them is
overwhelming....

#2111 LUC'S REVENGE Catherine George
Devastatingly attractive Luc Brissac was not only interested in
buying Portia's childhood home—scene of something so traumatic
she had blotted it from her memory—he was determined to have
Portia, as well! But when Luc took her back to France as his future
bride, the past went with them....

#2112 THE MISTRESS DECEPTION Susan Napier
When Rachel had innocently offered to undress Matthew Riordan
after a party, she didn't expect to find herself being blackmailed!
Matthew certainly wanted her as his mistress—but was he driven
by desire or deception?

#2113 A SUSPICIOUS PROPOSAL Helen Brooks
Millionaire businessman Xavier Grey seemed intent on pursuing
Essie. And he was used to getting what he wanted! But when he
proposed, was it an affair or marriage he had in mind...and could
Essie trust him?

#2114 AN INNOCENT AFFAIR Kim Lawrence
Everything had looked set for Hope's marriage to gorgeous tycoon
Alex Matheson—until the rumors started. As a top international
model, Hope was used to tabloid speculation. But now she *had* to
convince Alex of her innocence....

CNM0500